GLIMMER TRAIN STORIES

EDITORS
Susan Burmeister-Brown
Linda Davies

CONSULTING EDITORS
Scott Allie, Annie Callan, Dave Chipps

COPY EDITOR
Mark Morris

TYPESETTING & LAYOUT
Florence McMullen

COVER ILLUSTRATOR
Jane Zwinger

STORY ILLUSTRATOR
Jon Leon

FINAL-PAGE ILLUSTRATOR
Bernard Mulligan, Republic of Ireland

PUBLISHED QUARTERLY
in February, May, August, and November by
Glimmer Train Press, Inc.
812 SW Washington Street, Suite 1205
Portland, Oregon 97205-3216 U.S.A.
Telephone: 503/221-0836
Facsimile: 503/221-0837

©1994 by Glimmer Train Press, Inc. All rights reserved. No part of this periodical may be reproduced without the consent of Glimmer Train Press, Inc. The magazine's name and logo and the various titles and headings herein are trademarks of Glimmer Train Press, Inc. The short stories in this publication are works of fiction. Names, characters, places, and incidents are either the products of the authors' imaginations or are used fictiously. Any resemblance to actual events, locales, or persons, living or dead, is entirely coincidental. The views expressed in the nonfiction writing herein are solely those of the authors. *The Chicago Manual of Style* is used in matters of form.

Glimmer Train (ISSN # 1055-7520), registered in U.S. Patent and Trademark Office, is published quarterly, $29 per year in the U.S., by Glimmer Train Press, Inc., Suite 1205, 812 SW Washington, Portland, OR 97205. Second-class postage paid at Portland, OR, and additional mailing offices. POSTMASTER: Send address changes to Glimmer Train Press, Inc., Suite 1205, 812 SW Washington, Portland, OR 97205.

STATEMENT OF OWNERSHIP, MANAGEMENT, AND CIRCULATION. Required by 39 USC 3685, filed 9/24/94. Publication name: Glimmer Train, publication #10557520. Published quarterly (4x/yr). Publisher and owner: Glimmer Train Press, Inc. Complete mailing address of known office of publication and headquarters is 812 SW Washington St., #1205, Portland, OR 97205-3216. One year subscription price: $29. Editors and co-presidents: Susan Burmeister-Brown and Linda Davies, 812 SW Washington St., #1205, Portland, OR 97205-3216. Known bondholders: none. Extent and nature of circulation: a) average number of copies each issue during preceding 12 months, b) actual number of copies of single issue published nearest to filing date. Net press run: a) thirteen thousand, seven hundred seventy-five; b) sixteen thousand, seven hundred. Distributor sales: a) three thousand, ninety; b) three thousand, two hundred seventy-five. Paid or requested mailed subscriptions: a) six thousand, five hundred fifteen b) nine thousand, two hundred forty-three. Total paid/requested circulation: a) nine thousand, six hundred five; b) twelve thousand, five hundred eighteen. Free distribution by mail: a) one hundred; b) one hundred. Free distribution outside of mail: a) one hundred five; b) one hundred five. Total free distribution: a) two hundred five; b) two hundred five. Total distribution: a) nine thousand, eight hundred ten; b) twelve thousand, seven hundred twenty-three. Copies not distributed: a) five thousand, six hundred fifty-two; b) five thousand, seven hundred ninety-two. Copies returned from news agents: a) one thousand, six hundred eighty-seven; b) one thousand, eight hundred fifteen. Total sum of distributed and not distributed copies: a) thirteen thousand, seven hundred seventy-five; b) sixteen thousand, seven hundred. I certify that the statements made by me above are correct and complete—Linda Davies, Editor.

ISSN # 1055-7520, ISBN # 1-880966-12-3, CPDA BIPAD # 79021

DISTRIBUTION: Bookstores can purchase *Glimmer Train Stories* through these distributors:
Anderson News Company, 9632 Hwy. 20W, Madison, AL 35728
Bernhard DeBoer, Inc., 113 E. Centre St., Nutley, NJ 07110
Bookpeople, 7900 Edgewater Dr., Oakland, CA 94621
Ingram Periodicals, 1226 Heil Quaker Blvd., LaVergne, TN 37086
IPD, 674 Via de la Valle, #204, Solana Beach, CA 92075
Pacific Pipeline, 8030 S. 228th St., Kent, WA 98032
Ubiquity, 607 Degraw St., Brooklyn, NY 11217
SUBSCRIPTION SVCS: EBSCO, Faxon, READMORE

PRINTED IN U.S.A. ON RECYCLED, ACID-FREE PAPER. ♻
Subscription rates: One year, $29 within the U.S.
Airmail to Canada, $39; outside North America, $49.
Payable by Visa/MC or check for U.S. dollars drawn on a U.S. bank.

Attention short-story writers: We pay $500 for first publication and onetime anthology rights. Please include a self-addressed, sufficiently stamped envelope with your submission.
Send manuscripts in January, April, July, and October.
Send a SASE for guidelines, which will include information on our Short-Story Award for New Writers.

Dedication

We dedicate this issue with strong hopes
for the peace process in Ireland,
the land that brought us Siobhan Dowd and Bernard Mulligan,
whose crucial missives and charming inks
give special spirit to our pages.

This peace has been slow to find.
Many others are now in the making.
May they last.

And to Robert Xavier Rodriguez,
composer of *A Gathering of Angels—Bolero for Orchestra,*
a work so full of joy
that we may embrace another winter.

See you in spring.

Susan Burmeister-Brown
Linda Davies

Contents

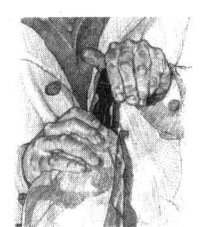

Elizabeth Oness
Rufus
7

Andrew Toos
First Novel
27

Victoria Lancelotta
A Proper Burial
29

Interview with E. Annie Proulx
She's "from away," but she got it right.
43

Lara Stapleton
Joselito
65

Pete Fromm
Helmets
77

Sleep
So now you know.
88

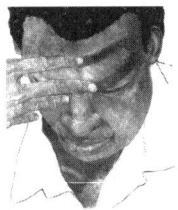

Tony Eprile
The Entrepreneurs
91

Contents

Article by Siobhan Dowd
Writer Detained: Ken Saro-Wiwa
108

Janice Levy
Blue Paper Napkin
113

Interview with Christine Turner
Improvisational comedian
126

George Rabasa
The Beautiful Wife
143

The Last Pages
159

Past Authors
167

I want to read them all!
168

Elizabeth Oness

This picture was taken by my father at the Shelburne Museum in Vermont. My sisters will laugh when they read this caption because my father took countless pictures of us at certain sites—and the Shelburne Museum is one of those places. My doll, Clarissa, was a prized possession and, as a child, I once wrote a story about how she was made and how I came to own her. People are, of course, much more complicated than dolls, and this seems to me one of the reasons we tell stories—to explain to ourselves the silences and vagaries of those we love.

Elizabeth Oness is a poet and fiction writer. A chapbook of her poems, *In the Blue before Night*, was published in 1991 by Heatherstone Press. Her stories have appeared in the *Hudson Review*, *American Short Fiction*, and the *1994 O. Henry Prize Anthology*. Oness is nearing completion of her first collection of stories, tentatively titled *Momentum*.

ELIZABETH ONESS
Rufus

A friend of Jonathan's had given him the car when he returned to the United States. It was a dented, gray Toyota with primer silvering the extensive rust and doors that didn't lock. After a year of traveling through Asia and New Zealand, Jonathan had returned to D.C. broke, and he found it an unexpected sign of adulthood that a friend his own age could afford this generosity. The doors that didn't lock hardly seemed to matter—until he found Rufus living in his car. Actually, Rufus didn't live in the car, he slept in it, but it seemed like the same thing. Jonathan's apartment was a few blocks from the men's shelter on Fourteenth Street, and he guessed that Rufus got his meals there. He didn't like to ask too many questions; somehow it seemed that the more he knew, the more responsible he was, that asking too many questions was like feeding a stray cat.

Jonathan found him in his car on a rainy night in October, a night when he was expected at his prospective in-laws for dinner. He opened the door of his car, then jumped back, startled by a substantial black man, in a paisley polyester shirt and a John Deere cap, sitting in the driver's seat, reading the newspaper. The man slapped the pages together and stared for a moment at the young Chinese man staring in at him. The scent of cologne floated into the damp air.

"Excuse me," Jonathan said. "What's going on here?"

ELIZABETH ONESS

"Just getting out of the rain." The man started to fold up his paper. His hands trembled as he aimed the newspaper's folded end at the side pocket of his blue vinyl Pan Am bag. With the paper secure, he braced one hand against the steering wheel and pulled himself around. "It's about dinnertime anyway." The man worked his jaw sideways as he guided his feet out of the car door. His square face sagged, as if the roundness of his cheeks had slipped down to his jowls.

Rain pelted the shoulders of Jonathan's jacket and he felt a few cold drops slide down inside his collar. He waited silently, holding the door like a chauffeur. When the man got clear of the car, he turned and shuffled away. His wide, high hips were crooked, flattened underneath.

Jonathan got into his car, dropping down too hard. The man had moved the seat back. He checked the glove compartment: registration, insurance, nothing was missing. Before pulling out, he looked in the rearview mirror and saw the man set his bag on the hood of a parked car; the man bent over the bag and reached into it, fishing for something.

Now he would be late, and Pamela's parents would smile as they wordlessly telegraphed their disapproval. Jonathan had always felt uneasy around them. Although Pamela still denied it, her parents had been visibly surprised when they discovered he was Chinese. At their first meeting, Mrs. Wallace's brittle gaiety couldn't hide her discomfort; she touched the softly lined skin of her neck and exclaimed about everything he said as if it were startlingly new. Pam's father offered him wine and inquired about his parents with a grave delicacy. Jonathan told them that his father, an American, was an attorney in San Francisco, and his mother, who lived in D.C., was an acupuncturist who treated drug addicts. They had heard of his mother; she was frequently written up in the newspapers. Jonathan tried to keep the conversation from lingering on her work; he found it hard to talk about his mother without making her sound eccentric.

Rufus

Pam's father seemed reassured to know that Jonathan had graduated from a prestigious university in the northeast. Their genteel formality made Jonathan imagine himself boisterous, raising his glass and saying, "Well, what do you think the kids will look like?" Instead, they held their wineglasses by the stem and spoke slowly. Pamela sat next to him and basked in her parents' approval when he mentioned his acceptance at SAIS, the School for Advanced International Studies in Washington. He imagined Pam's mother murmuring "State Department" over lunch to her friends. Ever since that night he felt that any Wallace family occasion combined the polite evaluation of a job interview with the ominousness of a doctor's appointment.

Since they'd become engaged, he felt even less at ease. He carefully avoided mentioning the neighborhood he lived in, one of the last renovated blocks east of Dupont Circle. Every day, Jonathan passed the men lined up outside the shelter. Some stood silently on the pavement, staring toward the head of the line; others smoked cigarettes and talked as any group of men might. One pale young man, with a fixed grin, often hopped around on the sidewalk, flapping his flannel-clad arms. Glimpsed for a moment, he might have been a man enjoying himself, telling a joke at a party, but the moment went on for too long, and the way he spun on the pavement made Jonathan think of a wobbling gyroscope. A slight man with wire-frame spectacles often sat on the church steps reading a book in the late afternoon. He looked like a dutiful merchant, passing a quiet hour with a book. Another man costumed himself in various street trash, and Jonathan had recently seen him wearing a shaggy carpet toilet-seat cover as a hat. He swept the pink mop off his greasy head, bowing to women in the street. "I salute you with my tiara," he said.

Jonathan assumed that the man he'd found in his car was simply disoriented; he'd discovered it unlocked and decided to wait out the rain. But the following week, when Jonathan

ELIZABETH ONESS

opened his car door, he found the man sorting papers: odd-shaped scraps were neatly arranged along the dashboard, and four piles of bank statements and cancelled checks had been placed in neat stacks on the passenger seat. Jonathan peered in at him and the man moved to cover his papers as if the wind would blow them away.

"Look, you just can't do this," Jonathan said.

"Sorry." He gathered up the piles and set them crosswise on top of one another. A cigarette burned in the ashtray.

"And I don't smoke, so I'd appreciate it if you wouldn't smoke in my car." Jonathan heard the edge of superiority in his voice and felt embarrassed; he sounded like a snotty kid. He also realized that he'd made a tactical error: by setting the boundaries of what he could and could not do, it sounded as if he were giving the man permission to use his car.

The man placed two of the smaller piles in a black address book. The leather was soft and shiny. He snapped a thick rubber band around the book to secure it, then put the other papers into his bag.

"Don't mean to hold you up, lost track of time." He got out of the car and straightened up slowly.

Jonathan watched him silently, trying to look stern, but the man wasn't looking at him so he didn't notice.

He was on his way to pick up Pamela, and when he got into his car, the lingering smell of cigarettes and cologne made him guess the man was spending a lot of time in it. Of course the logical step would be to move the car, but parking in Washington, set by zone, restricted him from moving it very far. He imagined the man searching for the car and finding it several streets away. He'd be ashamed of trying, and failing, to elude someone who was old and without a place to stay.

He'd been avoiding telling Pamela. Jonathan knew she'd have a decisive plan that he, in turn, would probably resist. Pamela had pretty, delicate features, and a high, wispy voice, but he had learned, early on, that her decisiveness was deeply ingrained. They had met two years ago, while she was studying for the bar exam. On their second date she'd made it clear that passing the bar was her main priority. He remembered her tone, as if she were expecting resistance, and when he told her that he'd been saving money for several years to take an extended trip to New Zealand and the Far East, he saw her redden slightly and fumble with a bracelet she was wearing. He was attracted to that softness beneath her imperious tone. Something about the delicacy of her gestures, the way she always seemed to be in motion, made him think of moving water. He quickly discovered that the current running through her wasn't an abundance of energy but a reluctance to be still, as if she needed to be busy to account for herself.

One night, after making dinner at his apartment, they went to bed, and in the interval between the first time they slept together and the time before he left, the balance of pursuit between them shifted. She seemed endlessly curious about him. In those first weeks, her questions about his growing up at the clinic, the years he'd spent in California with his father, made him feel as if the different parts of his past were beginning to coalesce. Usually he felt at the mercy of his environment. He was one person when he visited his mother at the clinic, and another when he was skiing with friends in Vermont. Pamela began to say how much she would miss him, and even though he liked to hear it, he was also glad that he would be away while she was preparing for the bar. She often woke up fretful, worrying about what she needed to study, as if his presence slowed her down. Her worrying, her need to accomplish things, was a trait that even her new vulnerability didn't ease. And so he had left, knowing she would probably be working in Washington when he returned, and that whatever was going to be between them would become apparent then.

In his absence she passed the bar, got a job with a large firm

ELIZABETH ONESS

downtown, and her letters, arriving on corporate letterhead in China or New Zealand, were mostly filled with the news that she was working sixty hours a week, she was tired, she missed him, she was making money and had no time to spend it. Jonathan held these letters in his hand and looked out to the line of the horizon and the sea, the houses thatched with grass, and felt a strange sense of wonder that in some months he would return to Washington and his life would resume a distinct and linear course.

He told her about the man living in his car on a Sunday morning as they lazed over doughnuts and the paper.

"Why doesn't he sleep in the shelter?" she asked.

"I don't know."

"Well, ask him. Then tell him he has to find somewhere else to sleep. If you don't, he'll be living in your car all winter," she said.

All afternoon Jonathan rehearsed, to himself, different ways of asking the man not to stay in his car. He would be firm and logical, but kind. He would talk to him, explain. When he went to his car, the man wasn't there.

The following week the man was sleeping in the driver's seat, one arm draped over his Pan Am bag. Jonathan opened the door and touched his shoulder cautiously.

"Hey, wake up, I have to go," he said.

The man opened his eyes, then closed them for a moment and stretched. Jonathan felt annoyed by his leisurely waking.

"Look," he said, "don't you have anywhere else to sleep?"

"Would I be sleeping here if I did?"

"What about the shelter?" Jonathan asked.

"You ever spent the night in a shelter?"

Jonathan just looked at him.

"Don't mind eating there, but it's no place to sleep. Everybody's got knives, they try to steal my bag—nobody gonna take my

Rufus

bag. Dirty, too. Junkies piss in the beds, piss in the corners. I like my whiskey, but I don't do no drugs."

Jonathan didn't know what to say. He stood in the street while the man shuffled near the gas pedal for his shoes, a pair of brown slip-ons with imitation horse bits on top.

"You can't keep sleeping in my car."

"All right, young man, I'll find myself another spot." Abruptly, he pulled himself out of the car. His shoes made a noise like slippers on the chilly pavement. When Jonathan slipped into the front seat, it was warm.

"What's your name?" he asked.

"Rufus. Rufus Williams."

Jonathan extended his hand through the window and they shook. Driving away, he hoped that Rufus would find somewhere else to sleep and that would be the end of it.

Two days later Jonathan found Rufus playing the radio in his car. "You said you'd find somewhere else to stay."

"I tried." Rufus got out of the car and set his bag on the pavement. "I just haven't located myself yet."

"Well, you have to find somewhere else. And you're going to run down my battery playing the radio like that."

They stood, facing each other. Jonathan imagined how Rufus must see him: a young Chinese man in his twenties, clean-shaven and well fed. Jonathan reached into the car and snapped off the radio. Standing in the street, Rufus started to cry.

"You listen to me, young man. I'm a veteran. I paid my way my whole life. I had the same apartment twenty-five years an' I paid my rent regular, but they got us all out 'cause they makin' it condos. I'm a veteran an' they put me on the street." He dug a handkerchief out of his pocket and wiped his eyes. "I got all my things in storage, two color TVs, big La-Z-Boy chair, but I got no place to put it."

"Don't you get a pension from the VA?"

ELIZABETH ONESS

"Hardly 'nough to live anywhere decent. Damn crackheads everywhere. I got cut visitin' my girlfriend last month."

His crying became a snuffling whine. Jonathan shifted his backpack, wishing he would finish.

"I know you got to use your car. I'm going down to the city to see about some tenant-assistance program. See where I am on the wait list. I used to have two cars, used to have a big old Caddy. Wouldn't want someone sleepin' in that."

The next evening they had a party to attend in Arlington. Pam was in a good mood, fussing over the wrapping for a birthday present, teasing him. She wore a short red dress, not too fancy, but the kind of dress that inspired him to open doors for her, help her with her coat. When Jonathan opened his car door, he saw Rufus leaning forward in the front seat, reading a paperback by the light of a street lamp.

"Evening," he greeted Jonathan. He marked his place carefully before putting the book in his bag and raising his bulk out of the car. Jonathan introduced them, and watched Rufus take Pam's reluctant, slender hand in his large one.

"Pleased to meet you, young lady." Rufus took off his cap.

"Are you living in this car?" Pamela's no-nonsense tone made Jonathan wince.

"I wouldn't call it living. I stay here when I can't find nowhere else."

"Well, a car's no place to live in winter," Pamela said.

"Can't argue with you there."

"You have to find somewhere more permanent to stay." Pamela pushed her hair back from her face; her gesture had the air of a challenge.

"She always do your talking for you?" Rufus looked at Jonathan and then back to Pamela: "Listen young lady, this's his car and we had this discussion, him and me. I don't see how it's any of your business. I don't like sleepin' in his car any more'n

Rufus

he likes it, but I'm tryin' to get myself located and there ain't much I can do. You got a ring on your finger? He ain't your husband; you got no legal claim on this car. This discussion is between him and me."

Rufus shouldered his bag, gave Jonathan a steady look, and headed down the street toward the church.

Pamela got into the car and slammed the door. "I can't believe him, getting self-righteous about sleeping in your car! It smells disgusting in here. You should fix the door and get a locksmith to make a key."

Jonathan didn't answer.

"Jonathan?"

"Look, obviously I've thought about that."

"Well, do it."

"Pamela, has it ever occurred to you to look at this a little differently? I don't like having him in my car, but I have a bed to sleep in, and mostly I sleep with you—I have two beds at my disposal. How can I deny him my car on a cold night? I mean, of course it's annoying, but it's not like he prevents me from using the car."

"God, I can't believe you." Pamela crackled the sheet of directions. They drove out of D.C. silently, then navigated Arlington's turning suburban streets, looking for house numbers under yellow porch lights. Jonathan imagined Rufus going to his car and finding himself locked out. He would stand in the road with his blue Pan Am bag at his feet, yanking at the chrome door handle, impatient and bewildered.

At the party Pam told the story about Rufus several times. Her telling of it made Jonathan sound indecisive and ineffectual. She moved through the party in her red dress, her long legs picking her way around a few people sitting on the floor. Jonathan decided that he wouldn't discuss Rufus with her anymore, but a few days later, when she asked about him, he didn't feel like lying either.

"Just fix the lock and get a key made, will you? Pretty soon you'll have a damn hotel in your car; it's getting cold out there," she said.

Jonathan was making dinner at her apartment and he wasn't in the mood to argue. He stirred the tomato sauce and poured himself another glass of wine. He believed that it wasn't good to get mad while preparing a meal: it would turn the sauce or spoil the food. It followed that arguing over dinner wasn't good either.

"Will you take care of it before the end of the week?"

"I'll do it when I feel like it," he said.

"You don't take charge of things, do you realize that? You let everything drift along until it bumps into some sort of conclusion."

He swirled the wine in his glass and stared at her through the reddish tint. She was right, but he didn't necessarily think this was a bad way to live. It was the weakness implied that bothered him.

"You make me sound so spineless. Do you know there are religions, whole belief systems, based on the idea of action in nonaction, allowing things to come to their natural conclusion?"

"Spare me that Eastern bullshit. It's just an excuse for not doing anything about it."

"Listen, it's fucking cold out there. What's he going to do when he gets to my car and he's locked out?"

"He'll find somewhere else. He doesn't have much incentive to look for a place if he knows he can drink all day and crash in your car at night."

"He doesn't always drink. He reads." Jonathan was uncomfortably aware of a strange internal echo. This sounded like something his mother would say.

"I can't believe you're defending him." Pamela stood in the center of the room holding two cloth placemats, her anger suspending her motion toward the table. "You can't spend your whole life just working around things you don't want to deal with."

"You're always so right." Jonathan set down the knife he was holding. He thought of the night of the party, of Pam telling the story over and over. It had been humiliating and he had let her get away with it. "You seem to thrive on this, you know?"

"What?"

"Arguing—it seems you're in the right profession." He saw her flinch, and knew the remark had hit home. He picked up his coat and walked out of her apartment, leaving the door wide open behind him.

He walked down Connecticut Avenue in the cool night air. How long had they been like this? Eastern bullshit. Underneath everything was that really how she felt? He knew that Pamela valued speed, efficacy; they had often talked about how they complemented each other. Walking down the street he realized that perhaps, without her knowing it, Pamela loved him for exactly what she criticized: he was malleable, easy to get on with. He would be in school, undisruptive, while she climbed the corporate ladder. What if he wanted to drop out of SAIS, move somewhere else? He tried to imagine it. Pamela would have a fit.

As he went over the argument in his mind, he remembered the disturbing feeling of echoing his mother's logic. He wasn't at all like her, but something in his reasoning had sounded implacable and familiar. The magazine and newspaper stories painted her as noble, but really she was just oblivious to the accepted way of doing things. It still amazed him that she and his father had ever been married. His father accomplished things by understanding the law, by knowing what series of precedents would allow him to position himself advantageously. His mother simply did things—without preparation, without money. Years ago, she had heard about a doctor in New York who was treating drug addicts with acupuncture. She took Jonathan out

ELIZABETH ONESS

of school for a few weeks and brought him to New York City, where he had trailed around the hospital after her, watching her place needles in the lobes of people's ears. Some of the patients gazed at him curiously; others ignored him. He had never seen so many colors of people. When she and Jonathan returned to D.C., a growing group of jittery patients came and sat in the waiting room along with those who came to be treated for back pain or tennis elbow. When one of the other acupuncturists complained that the detox patients made the other patients nervous, his mother simply opened her own clinic. She wasn't bothered by the fact that her patients couldn't pay, that she and Jonathan lived in two small, makeshift rooms above the clinic. His mother had found her mission. When he was away at college, she'd taken to walking through the back alleys of northwest D.C., quietly trying to convince people, mostly young girls, to come into the clinic for treatment. When he found out, he was furious with her, but she simply poured tea for him and smiled. "I do it in the daytime," she had said. "No one bothers me." He had not understood her at all then, but since returning from China his sense of what was possible had shifted.

Now he was hungry. He'd bought a bottle of red wine to drink with dinner and he wished that he'd taken it with him. He looked in restaurant windows as he walked down the street, but he didn't feel like paying to eat by himself. He stopped and bought a half dozen bagels and a container of cream cheese.

Walking past his car, he peered through the window. Rufus wasn't there.

"Lookin' for me?"

Jonathan turned to see him walking out of the alley. With a streetlight behind him, he looked kindly, paternal.

"I just got a bottle. Like to have a drink?"

"Sure."

Jonathan got into the driver's seat and Rufus walked around

to the other side.

"Woman trouble?" Rufus asked.

"How can you tell?"

"It's Saturday night and you got your dinner in a bag." He grinned at Jonathan and pulled a bottle of brandy out of a paper bag. Jonathan tried not to think about germs as he wiped off the top of the bottle. He didn't usually drink. A glass of wine every so often. He held the liquor in his mouth for a long moment before swallowing.

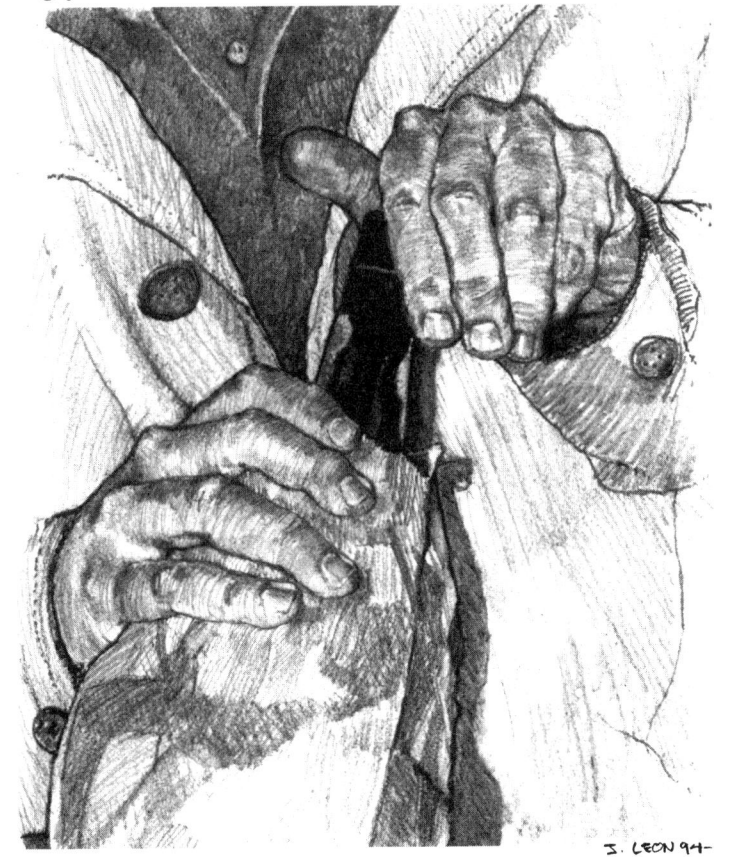

"Women like her are just like little kids," Rufus said. "They push you just to see how far you'll go. All you gotta do is tell them you had enough. They squawk a little, but they learn."

"Pam's got a mind of her own."

"I can tell," he laughed. "You got to watch out for a woman who thinks she knows what's best for you—that's the worst kind." He paused, took a drink. "No, there's worse. A woman that drinks is worse."

"Didn't you say you had a girlfriend?"

"Quit her. She'd get all liquored up, insensible. When I had my place, I kept a lock on the liquor cabinet. I told her she could drink all the beer she wanted, but I kept that cabinet locked up 'cause she'd get into the good stuff and it'd be gone."

Jonathan took a long drink and looked out at the night; the city sky was orange.

"You ever been married, Rufus?"

"Thirty-two years."

"You're kidding me." Jonathan turned to look at the outline of Rufus's face against the night. This single fact seemed to alter his silhouette. Rufus had been married longer than he'd been alive.

"Yep, thirty-two years. Cary was a lovely woman. Didn't drink, went to church regular, we got along real fine. She died eleven years ago in June and I'm just glad she ain't around now, 'cause she was a woman who believed in keepin' a nice house. Ain't no way she could live in a car, on the street."

They talked and drank into a blurry hour of the night. The next morning Jonathan woke with his shoes on, fully dressed. When he sat up in bed, he couldn't think what had happened for a moment. His throat felt hot and dry. He moved slowly into the kitchen for a glass of water and found one bagel left in the bag. He vaguely remembered Rufus cutting bagels with a knife, spreading cream cheese, joking that cream cheese was like white girls—you could see what you were doing in the dark.

Jonathan sat on the sofa with a glass of water and tried to reconstruct the evening. The red light on his answering machine blinked. He was sure it was Pamela, angry or apologetic. He remembered Rufus talking about women pushing at you, and he smiled at the blinking light. Good. But his head started to pulse in time with the tiny light, and the hot tightness in the back of his skull crept forward over his ears. He tried to piece together his conversation with Rufus, and for a moment the undividedness of it spilled back to him: two men sitting in a car, talking about women. Thirty-two years. Rufus Wilson had been married for thirty-two years. Now he would never get rid of him.

The phone rang and the sound seemed to press into his brain. He waited for the answering machine to rescue him. The caller hung up.

He didn't play back his messages until late in the afternoon. They were all Pamela, angry at first, then worried, then tearful. After a few calls, there were only dial tones.

He decided to let her stew for a while. When he finally did call, the following day, he told her that he was sick of being nagged at, and that it wouldn't be too difficult to find someone who was easier to get along with. The sound of his voice, still angry, surprised him.

"Will you come over later?" Her voice sounded teary.

"I have class until six. I'll come over then."

When she opened the door, he felt oddly formal. She offered him tea, and when he started to talk, she began to cry.

"We have to come to some agreement," he said quietly. "I don't want to have an ongoing argument about the way I live my life."

"I'm sorry, it just seems that—" she stopped herself.

She reached for him without saying anything else. He bent to kiss her and thought how this was the only thing that seemed uncomplicated between them. His fingers felt as if he were touching her through a thin layer of something cloudy, something she didn't see. They moved to her bedroom, but in bed his mind was too busy. He was distracted by odd thoughts, the radio, fragments of their argument. He tried to concentrate; he imagined her red dress. And what for her must have seemed like a deferral to her pleasure was for him strangely unconnected, as if he were observing her from a distance. Finally, he pulled away.

"This isn't right," he said.

"What?"

"That we fight and then do this."

"It's called making up," Pamela smiled.

"No, that's not what I mean."

"I was just angry the other night." Her voice was quiet, trying to soothe him.

"You were saying what you thought. Eastern bullshit. That's incredibly dismissive."

"Jonathan, I'm sorry. I was angry, I was being mean."

He pushed her hair back from her face. He didn't want to talk anymore.

That night, Jonathan found an empty McDonald's bag in his car. He felt annoyed and wondered if Rufus was inviting his friends to use the car. The next morning he went to his car primed for a serious discussion with Rufus. When he opened the door, he saw Rufus's Pan Am bag spilled on the passenger seat. He scrambled through the contents: an old brown shirt, a toothbrush and comb, a girlie magazine—no wallet, no papers, no knife. He stuffed everything back inside and set it gently on the car floor. He felt as if he'd stumbled onto a body. Had Rufus been mugged in the car? He hurried to school, sweating, and thought of what Rufus had said about the shelters. A friend at school suggested he call the VA hospital.

After class he found a pay phone and he waited as the operator transferred him between different units. He repeated his questions and waited on hold, suspended in a network of faint voices.

Rufus

Finally they located Rufus in intensive care: his condition was listed as stable. When Jonathan hung up the phone he felt relieved and a little sick.

After a few days, Jonathan started to worry. What if they discharged Rufus and he came back? The only thing worse than having a homeless man in his car would be having a sick homeless man in his car. He imagined carting Rufus around because he didn't have the heart to put him out on the street. He called to ask about visiting hours.

"You're visiting him?" Pam's voice was shrill with disbelief.

"I just want to make sure they know he doesn't have anywhere to live. I don't want them to release him and have him end up in my car."

Pamela started to speak, stopped, then took a deep breath.

"Jonathan, visiting him is absurd. You'll just develop more of a... relationship with him. And then he'll be *more* likely to come back."

Jonathan turned to look out the window. He felt enormously tired.

"You usually take the path of least resistance. It would seem to be easiest to let him go," Pamela said.

"You make me sound like a fucking jellyfish. I'm just trying to avoid having him come back sicker than he is."

"You're acting out of liberal guilt and you should just stop. It's not your fault that he's homeless. Are you going to turn into your mother?"

"There's nothing I want less than to be like my mother. She's completely eccentric; I'm just trying to be decent. You know, Pamela, once you decide how you feel about something, all you think about is how you can make your point. You don't even consider another perspective."

Pam's lip quivered. "Is this how you're planning to live your life? You're broke, in graduate school, and you're going to

Elizabeth Oness

encourage this man?"
"I just want to let someone know what his situation is."
"Fine." Pamela turned and walked into her bedroom.
Jonathan stood still. He imagined what it would be like not to have to explain or defend himself, not to expend any effort in understanding how their lives could mesh. He tried to think if he had anything of value in her apartment. He went to the hall closet, took his coat, and let himself out the door. He closed it quietly, finally, behind him.

The Washington Hospital Center was a vast complex of gray concrete buildings. The signs pointing to different roads and hospitals made him feel as if he were driving to an airport. He glanced around him as he walked in the front door—a TV in the lobby, people in wheelchairs, no one too frightening looking. At the information desk, he learned that Rufus was out of intensive care. As the nurse recited the directions to his room, Jonathan listened carefully; he didn't want to see anything he didn't need to.

He paused at the door of the unit. No one noticed him because no one seemed capable of lifting his head. The beds looked like half-prone chairs with canopies of tubes and bottles suspended over each one. In the near corner, a nurse with platinum-blond hair was drinking coffee and eating a muffin.

"Ah, excuse me, I'm here to see Mr. Williams," he whispered.
"Rufus?" she smiled. "He's right over there."
"I'd like to talk to you for a minute first, if I could."
"Sure, honey." She pointed to an orange stool next to her. He liked the way she said *honey*, not flirtatious, but reassuring. She was large and clean; he felt like a small child.

"I'm here because Rufus was living in my car. He has no place to go and I thought the hospital should know that. I don't want him to leave here and come back to my car."

"Of course not." She smiled at him as if this were just one of many small events in her day. "Mr. Williams is going to be here quite a while. As a matter of fact, he'll be having another operation in a week or two. He'll probably be up on the list for subsidized housing by the time he's ready to leave."

Jonathan stared at her for a moment; he felt amazed at some small order in the world.

He walked over to Rufus, who seemed shrunken inside his skin. Tubes containing different colors of fluids were patched into his arms and his sides. He had no idea what to say. The nurse came up behind him.

"Look who's here, Mr. Williams."

Rufus opened his eyes and smiled weakly. He tapped the plastic shell that covered his trunk. His head was set in a brace; he looked like a brown turtle with tubes.

"Look pretty funny, I bet." His voice was a croaking whisper.

"Yes, you do," Jonathan said. There was no getting around it.

"Pinched a nerve in my neck." He paused. "An' somethin' else, too."

Jonathan wasn't sure what to say about the "something else," if he should ask or not. "Well, they look like they're taking good care of you."

"Good TV," Rufus croaked.

Jonathan looked up at the large color TV suspended from the ceiling. "I should have brought you a present, but I forgot," he said. He sat down on the chair beside Rufus. There was a game show on TV, and the contestants, all fat and manic, bounced behind their lecterns like overexcited children. He was relieved when Rufus dozed off.

Jonathan picked himself up quietly and walked toward the door. He thanked the nurse, who smiled at him as if his visiting a man who had been sleeping in his car were the most normal thing in the world.

He hurried down the hall. In the elevator he had to wait for a man with tiny, shrunken legs to wheel himself in. Jonathan

ELIZABETH ONESS

forced a thin smile; the man stared back, sullen.

In the lobby Jonathan fished for his keys in his backpack; the double glass doors seemed like a finish line. Inside the first set of doors was a brightly lit candy machine, and it seemed incongruous there for some reason. Standing in front of the bright assortment of candies, he suddenly wanted to taste something very sweet. He dug in his pockets for change, chose a chocolate bar, and passed through the doors. Outside, he looked around him and realized the view was unfamiliar; it wasn't the way he'd come in. In the distance, beyond a parkway, a line of bare trees looked soft against the pale sky. He sat on a low concrete wall to get his bearings, to taste the sweetness in the cold morning air.

"And this is the wall I stared at while writing my first novel."

Victoria Lancelotta

It's difficult to see in this photo, but I'm sitting on a bearskin rug. My mother, though, was kind enough to allow me to keep my clothes on.

Victoria Lancelotta was born and raised in Baltimore, Maryland, where she attended Johns Hopkins University. She received her M.F.A. at the University of Florida, Gainesville, where she also taught fiction writing. Her story "Immediate Family" appeared in the spring 1994 issue of the *Crescent Review*. Lancelotta is at work on her first collection of short stories.

VICTORIA LANCELOTTA
A Proper Burial

My mother sits in front of me in a pressed white blouse and a tweed skirt. Her shoes are off because we're just home from the funeral, but she's left her stockings on. There is a small run in one of the toes. She's holding a drink in her hand, steady; the ice does not clink against the side of the glass at all. She's in front of me, still, and she drinks from the glass and my father is dead, was killed, in fact, on his way home from the supermarket where he had gone for bread three nights ago.

She moves to the chair by the fireplace and balances her glass on the arm, stares into the empty fireplace. The chair is tweed, like her skirt. She rests her feet on the ottoman. The run in her stocking seems to have grown in this short time.

I make a drink for myself in the kitchen. There are two bottles on the counter, gin and vermouth, and the cabinet with the glasses stands open. The countertops are covered with casserole dishes, sealed tight with Saran Wrap or foil; we have run out of room in the refrigerator. Its shelves are packed with dishes similar to these, platters of cold cuts and cheese cubes, olives. The next-door neighbor has brought two loaves of bread, one light and one dark, fresh baked.

Over the next weeks my mother and I box my father's things,

VICTORIA LANCELOTTA

his clothes and shoes and the tools from the garage. We pack them in cardboard boxes for the Salvation Army; we label them with black permanent marker—socks and ties, sweaters, suits. I go out on dates, with boys who are too old for me, but my mother says nothing. When I come home nights the house is dark, and I step around the boxes piled in the front hallway. My mother is asleep in the chair by the fireplace with her shoes off and an afghan over her legs, like a little girl up past her bedtime. Or, if not there, I find her on her bed with the spread only pulled past the pillows. She is never under the blankets, at least not since he died. These nights, I stand in the doorway and watch her while she sleeps, her hair sticky on her forehead.

Mornings, she is up before me, standing at the stove frying bacon in a skirt and slip, her blouse still unbuttoned, the cooling iron sitting near the sink. Her shoes and stockings are on and her hair is neat, the skin of her face white and papery as though she has not slept at all. She asks me if I will be home after school and I say no, that there are yearbook meetings, band rehearsals, and she smiles and sets my breakfast in front of me as if she's forgotten that I have not been in the band for years and have never mentioned the yearbook until now.

What I do after school is go downtown to Stiles Street, where there are secondhand-clothing stores and a corner bar with glass-brick windows whose bartender has never thought to ask me for an identification card. I understand that I look older than I am, and that this is a recent happening.

The bar is one room, small, not much bigger than our living room at home, with an L-shaped counter, stools, and two red vinyl booths in the middle of the small floor. There are red plastic baskets of peanuts on the counter and tables and, in huge Mason jars lined up in the corner by the cash register, pickled cucumbers, onions, and eggs, fifty cents apiece. I sit at the second stool from the door, which is tied open with green plastic clothesline to let in air that smells like rush hour and the fish market down

A Proper Burial

the street. There's enough light at that end of the bar for me to spread my books out and study, and I usually get a can of beer and a pickled onion to go with it. The onion I eat by layers, vinegar stinging under my ragged thumbnails. The bartender serves me and goes back to his place at the other end of the bar, with his newspaper and a small black-and-white TV. By about four-thirty, people start coming in, older men with metal lunch buckets from the steel mill and sometimes men in suits and ties, coming in on their way out of the city, home. These men look at me sometimes, but mostly not, or only briefly, and some of them I am beginning to recognize. And I pile my books into my bag, put money on the counter, and leave, and sometimes on my way to the bus stop I go into the secondhand stores. They are bright, yellow with fluorescent lights, brighter than outside, and I am convinced that one day I will be looking at sweaters, maybe, or belts, and I will pick one up and it will be my father's.

My mother meets a man named Robert, who wears a diamond ring on his pinky and has more hair than my father did. She invites him for dinner and asks me that morning if I could please skip band practice and come straight home after school to help her clean the house. Although the house is clean, I say yes.

When I get home, she is there already. She has left work early and had her hair set and is laying a fire. There is bark and soot on her bathrobe.

"Nina, honey, can you vacuum in here?" She stands and brushes herself off. She says, "Don't be upset that Robert is coming, Nina. He's just a friend. He's someone I can talk to. I'll always love your father, Honey," she says, "so don't worry about that."

Her eyes are dull and gray. I am not, in fact, worried about that, about Robert and my father. I cannot decide whether I'm worried about my mother or myself, but I think that there is not much of a difference either way. I go to her and kiss her cheek,

VICTORIA LANCELOTTA

and there is the taste of sweat and face cream.

My mother has set out flowers and candles, and a white cloth on the kitchen table. The fabric is heavy, curtainy. There is a large roast at the center of the table surrounded by small, shiny vegetables. There is a gravy boat that matches the candlesticks in design; there is bread in a woven basket with a cloth napkin thrown over it. My mother and I are both in simple black dresses, she with pearls and I with large silver earrings that are making, I think, too much noise. Robert pours wine and raises his glass.

"A toast," he says, "to the loveliest dinner companions I've had in a long time." His eyes go from me to my mother and back to me. I wonder if he thinks we are in mourning. Robert talks to my mother about the property values in our neighborhood and I take my earrings off and lay them next to my plate.

As we eat, I notice the tablecloth becoming wrinkled around the bottoms of the dishes and the drips and splatters of gravy, small and deliberate looking. When Robert is finished, I take his plate.

"So you'll be graduating this year, Nina. Any plans?" His voice is loud in the close air.

"Not yet, really," I say.

"College?"

"Nina's never been much for planning ahead," my mother says. She does not look to me like a woman on a date. Her face is shiny through the powder she put on and pieces of her hair have come undone, damp in the kitchen heat. There is spilled wine by her glass. Her voice is tired.

I clear the table and set out their coffee cups, with sugar and milk in bowls that match the candlesticks and also the gravy boat in the sink.

"You're not having any, Nina?" Robert says, turning the ring on his little finger.

"No, I—actually have a date." I look at my mother. "I should

A Proper Burial

really get ready now, if that's all right."

"On a school night?" Robert says.

My mother is smiling, her eyes heavy, focused, I think, on a spot between the two of us.

"It's a study date," I say. I lean to kiss my mother's shiny cheek. "I won't be late." I reach to shake Robert's hand, but he pushes his chair back and stands, quick, so quick for such a big man, takes my hand in both of his and kisses me, his lips just touching the corner of mine.

"Have a good time," he says. "Be careful." He sits again and faces my mother, who has poured the last of the wine in her glass and twirls it in the vague candlelight.

In the hallway, I brush my hair and straighten the seams of my dress, which are frayed, pulled tight from being shrunk in the wash. I put on lipstick, what the girls at school call fuck-me red, and run down the front steps when I see the headlights in the driveway.

The boy tonight is named Roy, and he smokes while he drives. His right hand is on my thigh. He says we will go to the liquor store and then to the park, as long as I'm not too cold. I tell him I'm not.

"The only problem with girls your age is that you can't go to bars with them," he says, and squeezes my leg. We park in the side lot of the liquor store so the clerks can't see me in the car. Roy goes in and I check my hair in the rearview. I think about

Victoria Lancelotta

the bar on Stiles Street, my stool by the door with a tear in the vinyl, where I rip at the threads while I study. I think about telling Roy to go there. He comes back with a paper bag.

"Beer okay?" he says.

"Fine," I nod. "Let's go."

It is cold, and Roy runs the heater in the parked car. He throws the empty cans in the back seat, pitches his cigarettes out the window, and tells me that I should go to college when I finish school.

"College was the best time I've had," he says. "I wish I had the money to go back and finish."

"Money's something," I say. I slide across the seat closer to him and he pulls his jacket around both of us. He kisses my hair, my eyes; I picture Robert doing these things to my mother in our living room in front of the fire she laid, but it is getting late and she is probably walking him to the door now, and I pull away from Roy.

"I have homework."

"Now?" he says, surprised.

"My grades," I say, "I have to keep my grades up if I want to go anywhere next fall."

He shrugs, kisses me on the cheek, and puts the rest of the beer in the back seat. He takes me home, drives the speed limit, and kisses me again in our driveway, his cold hand moving farther up my thigh, under my skirt. He says he'll call me on Friday. Roy is one of the nicer ones.

Robert is gone, and the candles on the kitchen table have burned down to stubs of lumpy wax. My mother is in the living room, sleeping on the chair in front of the dying fire. There are two empty brandy snifters on the hearth. Her hair has come undone; wiry gray strands are loose around her forehead and a pin has fallen to the front of her dress. Moving toward her, for the hairpin, I see her hands, gripping the arms of the chair; in her

A Proper Burial

sleep, her knuckles are white.

In the kitchen, after loading the dishes from the sink to the dishwasher and pouring the milk from the bowl on the table back into the carton, I scrape the wax from the tablecloth, then wad it up for the laundry.

Upstairs, the hall light is on, the bedroom doors open. My parents' bed is made, the spread smooth, tight.

On Fridays, to celebrate the end of the week, I order whiskey-and-soda instead of beer, and sometimes a pickle along with the onion. It is when I order the whiskey that I think the bartender might say something to me, something like How old are you, anyway? But he doesn't. He just nods and brings me the drink with extra napkins to wipe the pickle vinegar from my fingers. It is getting dark earlier, and cold, and the door is not propped open so much anymore. On Fridays, also, the men begin coming in a little earlier and they talk more, and louder, and leave bigger tips. Some of them have begun to say hello to me, and others just nod. A few who wear hats have tipped them, but mostly the hats are torn and grease-stained.

I have never seen a woman in this place. I wonder if some of the men don't go home to have dinner and change and then bring their wives back, after I'm gone. They would have teased hair, the wives, and tight skirts and long nails, painted for a night out. And perfume, I think, and the smell of it would be choking in this small room.

My mother goes out with Robert twice a week, or three times, and says that she will invite him for Thanksgiving dinner. Robert's ex-wife and their children live in town, but they are not on good terms. He does not see his children as often as he'd like, sometimes not even on holidays. He has two sons, and a daughter my age who goes to a private school. He says he would like me to meet her, that he thinks we would get along. He says

Victoria Lancelotta

also that she knows a lot of boys, his daughter, that she knows nice ones who will be going to good colleges next year, Ivy League even, and that maybe he could arrange for a double date. My mother smiles at this, says it is a good idea. My mother smiles more often. She makes elaborate meals when Robert is over.

The week before Thanksgiving she has her hair dyed, the same dark blonde as mine, with highlights to cover the gray. She says it is the color her hair was when she was younger. She spends time arranging it at the mirror in the hallway, and I find strands of it on the table where she leaves her purse and keys. She says that the older I get, the more alike we look. She asks if I would like to invite a date for Thanksgiving dinner, also. Roy says he will come.

That week, we go shopping, my mother and I, and I choose a bright red dress. My mother says it's a good color for the holidays, and besides, it sets off her new hair, so she buys one in the same color. She takes me to the salon for a trim and offers to get me highlights, too. I tell her I'll think about it. While she pays, I go to the drugstore and buy a box of cheap peroxide.

At home, I tell her I'm going to take a bath and study before dinner. I lock myself in the bathroom and follow the directions on the box of bleach; I leave it on a few extra minutes for good measure. By the time I'm done, my hair is white, almost transparent, my eyes suddenly darker and bruised looking.

"Your hair," my mother says at dinner, and her hand goes to her own, to the careful waves. "What have you done?" she says. Her mouth is trembling; lipstick is faded in the lines around it.

"I dyed it myself."

"You look like a slut," she says. "It's bad enough you act like one, but to look like this? Why? Why did you do this?"

We are sitting across the table from one another. There are no candles or flowers in our way.

"Look at yourself," she says. Her eyes are glazed, glassy with

A Proper Burial

tears. "Why are you doing this to me? What were you thinking?" She drops her hand to the table and a fork clatters to the floor; the tears are running down her face, dropping on her shirt. "You—you—" she says, shaking her head as if she is not sure what will come next. "Do you know what your father did to me? Do you know how many affairs he had, how many women? Are you stupid?" she says, her voice quiet, amazed. Her face is blotchy, swollen, streaked with makeup. "Are you doing this to me because you're stupid?"

"I'm not stupid," I say.

"No," she says, and stands, her hip knocking against the table. Her glass rolls to the floor; it crunches under her feet. "I can't look at you. I can't look at you."

She leaves and I pick up the fork and sweep the glass into a pile, as much of it as I can, and I leave the pots warming on the stove in case she's hungry later. When I go upstairs, she's in the tweed chair. She doesn't look at me when I walk past.

Robert carves the turkey; Roy loads stuffing onto plates, and my mother and I sit, in our red dresses, princesses across the table. She wears the silver earrings that I had taken off, lost track of; they jingle and her eyes shine. She does not look at me. Robert tells me that my hair is beautiful. Roy lays his hand on my thigh. We say grace; we eat slowly; the conversation is polite, civilized. Roy and I are the ones to clear the table and, as I take the plates away, I see my mother staring at the wall, at the clock on the wall, her eyes glazed, stunned.

"You still have so much," Robert says, covers her hand with his. His diamond flickers in the candlelight.

Roy is at the sink, his back turned, and my mother looks at me suddenly, her eyes sharp, deadly, and I realize I'm holding my breath because, for the first time, I think my mother is seeing something, something old, older than I am in the lines of my face and the set of my chin, something that does not belong to me,

Victoria Lancelotta

nor to her. She takes her hand from Robert and the sound of water running in the sink is very loud, suddenly, and the clink of silverware also, and I would speak, but my voice is my father's voice and I am afraid to hear it coming from my own mouth, my mouth that is so like my father's.

Robert watches us.

"Roy," he says, his eyes never leaving my face, "you can bring that other bottle of wine over."

We eat the dessert, the civilized conversation continues. Robert is solicitous to my mother, who is trying hard, very hard, it seems, to be gracious without acknowledging my presence at the table at all. There are drops of sweat on her upper lip and she blots them with her napkin, allows Robert to squeeze her hand between forkfuls of pie, keeps her eyes focused on her plate as if she is afraid to look up and see who sits at her table. And Robert watches me, searches my face for this thing that makes my mother want to scream and cry, as though he would strike it out if he could see it, but he can't; there is nothing for anyone but my mother to see.

I hold my napkin in front of my mouth, as much as I can. Roy and Robert watch me.

"Is there something wrong with your mouth, Nina?" Roy says.

"I'd like more wine, please, Robert," my mother says, and stands, goes into the bathroom in the hall, and slams the door.

We continue as though nothing has happened. We put the leftovers in the refrigerator and the plates in the dishwasher. Roy asks if I would like to go for a drive and I tell him that, tonight, I think I should stay here. The bathroom door is still closed, locked, and no sound comes from behind it. None of us knocks.

When Roy leaves, I sit in the living room with Robert. There are two brandy snifters on the table by the couch; the tweed chair

A Proper Burial

is empty, and there is a crack of light under the bathroom door. He pours brandy, hands a glass to me, and we sit, next to each other on the couch. I kick my shoes off, prop my feet on the table, and Robert does the same.

"She's still in there," I say.

Robert nods.

"I'm sure she's fine," I say. "Or she'll be fine soon." I drink and put the glass on the table, by my feet.

"Don't you miss your father, Nina?" he says.

I look at him in profile, this big man, still handsome, I can see, in an expensive suit, his tie loosened.

"Of course I miss my father," I say, but the question is almost strange to me. I have not thought about my father. It is my mother I think of, in the chair at night, or on the big neat bed, with her pretty hair and empty eyes. I am suddenly tired.

"Your mother needs you, Nina," Robert says. His big hand is on my shoulder, squeezing it gently. "Be patient with her," he says, and now the hand is on my neck, light for all its size and warmth, and the fingers are threading through my hair. My breath is coming quick, and there is still no sound from the bathroom.

"Your mother must have looked just like you," he says, stroking my hair, my neck, and now my cheek, tracing my lips with his thumb. I am absolutely still. I am watching him now, his face, and I know that behind him in the front hall is the door to the bathroom with the crack of light beneath it and behind that is my mother.

"You're both very beautiful," he says, so quiet, so that my mother might not hear, and if she walked out now she would see nothing wrong; she would see a man touching her daughter's cheek as an uncle might; she would see her daughter's slut-blonde hair, but what is wrong with that?

"I look like my father," I say, and his thumb is in my mouth, the ball of it against my bottom teeth as if testing how sharp they

Victoria Lancelotta

are. The thumb moves gently back and forth, squeaking against the edges of my teeth; it tastes of turkey and cologne, and the other fingers rest on my cheek.

"And my daughter looks just like me," he says. He traces his thumb down my chin, my neck, along my collarbone to the neckline of my dress. I feel the damp trail of my own saliva and hear the bathroom door open.

My mother comes into the room and stands, the front of her dress damp, her makeup wiped off and her hair scraped back flat, facing us. Robert's hands rest easily in his lap. I wipe my chin. My mother's mouth opens, closes soundlessly. She turns to go upstairs; she's left the bathroom light on.

I am on my stool, second from the door, and the bartender comes to take my order but hesitates, squinting, and I think: Now he'll ask; he'll ask for my driver's license; he'll tell me to leave and not come back, and I feel my cheeks getting hot and red, but he says, "You dyed your hair."

"I did," I say.

He smiles, pleased with himself. "Beer and an onion?" he says, and I nod.

In my bag is a stack of college brochures, shiny colored paper folded in thirds, and I try to imagine my picture on the front of them, walking along a path filled with leaves, orange and red, because it is always autumn at these places, or so the pictures say.

The door is closed and there is a heater running in the corner, but the room is still cold and damp, and outside is a rain that will change to snow, probably, by nightfall. The men come in, scraping their shoes on the floor for traction, shivering a little.

"Honey? This is for you," the bartender says, surprising me, setting a steaming mug down in front of me. He nods over my shoulder. "It's from him over there," he says.

I turn in my stool and see a man, at the other end of the bar;

A Proper Burial

he raises his own glass to me in a toast. He is wearing a suit, and an overcoat; he is older than Roy, though not as old, for instance, as Robert. When the bartender walks away, he comes and stands next to me.

"It's an Irish coffee," he says. "They're good when it's cold like this."

"Thanks," I say. "I've never had one."

He raises his eyebrows. "Never? Really?" He looks as though he will ask me something else, but he smiles and says, "Well. If you like it, we'll get more."

His hair is light and carefully combed, his smile brilliant. His face would have been fine on one of my brochures, maybe twenty years ago. He sets his glass on the bar and his nails are manicured, perfect; there is fine, blond hair on the back of his hand. The Christmas lights in the window glint red and green on the narrow gold of his wedding band.

"Can you excuse me?" I say. My voice is in a tunnel, a jar. "I'll just be a minute."

I slide off the stool. I leave my things and, across the bar, I see the ladies' bathroom door. I latch it behind me, turn the lights on. It is a small room, no stalls, just a room with a toilet and sink, painted a sick yellow that was once probably bright, but the paint has chipped and faded, peeled from the walls, and they are covered in writing, the walls, some of it also faded but some fresh—so women *do* come here, after all, women besides me.

In the mirror, my face is also yellow, and the roots of my hair are coming in already. They seem darker than before, and my eyebrows darker, also, over my father's eyes and my father's nose, but I can't look at myself, so I look at the walls, but the words are some foreign language, the letters jumbled, unreadable.

In the corner, I crouch on my heels, my arms around my knees, and I try to keep my eyes closed, but sometimes they open, making sure I am still here in this warm, closed room, and

Victoria Lancelotta

from the other side of the door, I hear the voices, the men's voices, but the door is solid between us and there is no one who will knock.

E. ANNIE PROULX
She's "from away," but she got it right.

Interview
by Michael Upchurch

With a mere three books published over a five-year period, Vermont-based writer E. Annie Proulx has established herself as an engagingly potent voice in American fiction. Her debut, Heart Songs and Other Stories (1988), took a wry, flinty look at backwoods life in her home state, while her first novel, Postcards (1992), led readers on a cross-country trek with protagonist Loyal Blood, a murderer on the run, who never imagines that the family he left behind might change during his forty-year absence. Postcards went on to win the 1993 PEN/Faulkner Award for Fiction, the first time the prize ever went to a woman.

E. Annie Proulx

Proulx followed this with The Shipping News *(1993), a seriocomic tale about a widowed newspaper hack named Quoyle (the name derives from a ship-deck spiral coil of rope designed to be "walked on if necessary"), who tries to remake his life in the fictional fishing community of Killick-Claw on Newfoundland's Great Northern Peninsula. Reviewers' praise, followed by four major literary prizes—National Book Award, Pulitzer Prize, Heartland Prize from the Chicago Tribune, Irish Times* International Fiction Prize*—soon*

Glimmer Train Stories, Issue 13, Winter 1995
©1994 Michael Upchurch

Interview: E. ANNIE PROULX

launched Proulx onto the best-seller lists. Even Newfoundlander Patrick O'Flaherty, writing in Toronto's Globe and Mail, *conceded that, though she was "from away," she got her Newfoundland setting exactly right.*

With all the attention she is getting, one might expect Proulx to be either full of herself or overwhelmed by the pressures of a months-long media onslaught. Instead, she is a gracious soul with a ready sense of humor and an eager appetite for talk about books and fiction.

Rather than resembling one of the more rustic characters in her work, she has the air of a mischievous professor intent on upsetting as many apple carts as possible, just to see what the aerodynamic possibilities of apples might be. Proulx does have an extensive academic background, with an M.A. degree followed by doctoral research in Renaissance economic history, the Canadian north, and traditional China, and her novels, purely intuited though they may feel, owe much in their writing method to Proulx's long immersion in the library stacks. Before doing any on-the-spot research for a book, she likes to read about its setting first, turning to volumes on folklore, history, etymology, horticulture, and botany—"so at least I'll know what I'm looking at."

"I love scholarship," she explains, adding that the preliminary drafts of her novels are sprinkled with footnotes (later eliminated) which identify the sources of various details in the book.

UPCHURCH: *What other kinds of research do you do? Any formal interviews with people in the places you plan to write about?*
PROULX: Never formal interviews, but what is useful is eavesdropping, listening, talking to people in an informal way, sitting around tables swapping stories, listening to kids. I might take notes, too. And I keep huge notebook-sketches. I have one that's just physical descriptions: faces, postures, walks, the way somebody's elbows point outward, their complexion, the cast of their eyes, any scars, pockmarks, peculiar gaits, accents, odd ways of holding the mouth.

So all these things I'll write down at odd moments as I travel.

She's "from away," but she got it right.

And then, later, I'll tear those pages out and put them in the character notebooks, so if I need a character I can look through what are now literally hundreds and hundreds of physical descriptions of people of all ages and sizes. There I have this data bank of characters waiting to be used. And when I approach a new novel, I know the characters I want and will look through to see if I can find a physical description that fits.

I also work a lot from photographs, especially when I'm doing something that is set in a particular period. I'll spend weeks with books of photography from the period and place, and study them very carefully, again to get the right kind of bone structure and build and clothing.

How did you manage to write The Shipping News *so quickly, then?*
It was two years. That wasn't quick.

Well, it seems quick to me.
I've been putting off fiction writing for a long time, so I'm in something of a hurry. I'm an omnivorous reader and I'm a hard worker, so, usually, I do all the reading first. I know the story I want to do, then I'm off and up there and working on details. The story's already set in mind, so it's just a question of getting the details and the small bits.

Does the story in mind come from blind research—reading things on a landscape or culture, and deciding you'd like to write about it?
No, no. I don't know how to explain this. I've been told it's not an ordinary approach to things. I just have a stack of novels in my head, waiting to be written. I've got three there now, and I think of them as boxes wrapped in brown paper and tied with twine. And when I'm ready to write them, I can more or less mentally untie them and go at it. I try not to think of them at all until I'm ready to start work. And the story is there, complete. I have the whole thing when I start out. Don't ask where it comes from, because I don't know. It's just that something clicks over and then I've got the whole thing I want to do.

I don't start doing the research until I know what I want to do.

Interview: E. ANNIE PROULX

For example, I'm piling up stuff I know that I'll need on the book that I do after the one I'm working on now. I've been compiling the materials for a couple of years now: books and papers and photographs and odds and ends.
This is for the book that will follow Accordion Crimes *[Proulx's third novel, in progress]?*
Yes. So, in a sense, I'm working on that now in a low-key kind of way. But usually the ideas for the stories come in a great mad rush when I'm finishing something, finishing a piece of writing, on the final pages of the last draft, after you're working on it and working on it, and you're sick unto death of it, and it's just the last little bit. At that time, you're so damned fed up with the thing you'll do anything. Your mind is racing around madly, thinking anything would be better to write than this. Anything at all! A grocery list would be better to write. And then, of course, all kinds of marvelous ideas for books unwritten come into mind.
Do they come and go?
No, they come to be selected—or rejected. That's how *The Shipping News* came, and definitely how *Accordion Crimes* came: just in a quick click.
How much experience had you had of Newfoundland before writing The Shipping News?
I went up there five or six years ago to go fishing. It had been in the back of my mind to go there for fifteen years before that. I went up with a friend, dragged up the canoes and so forth, and the minute I got my hands on a map I fell madly in love with the place-names, which were extraordinary, just extraordinary! And stories began jumping off the map at me. A place with such a name as Joe Batt's Arm or the Fogo Islands or the Topsail Mountains or the Annieopsquotch Mountains. Or a place that has a train called the Newfie Bullet.
All these place-names carried stories that seemed to jump at me. So a year or so later, as I was finishing up *Postcards*, the idea for *The Shipping News* came to me, all of it hung on a guy that

She's "from away," but she got it right.

I'd seen on the ferry. There was a man on the ferry who was coming back from the mainland, and he was drunk and he stayed up all night. Skinny guy with red hair and violet-colored plastic sandals: women's sandals. And he sang all night long while everyone around him was trying to go to sleep. He sang about not being able to find a job, and coming back, and what was the use, and so forth, in this very low voice.

I was seated right behind him. I could hear it fairly well, found it fascinating, wrote some of it down. So he was in mind to work into this story about shipping news. I wanted to write about the fact that there were no jobs and that the fishery was collapsing and unfolding and falling down. And, actually, he evaporated from the story. Only his plastic sandals stayed in, with the guy who sells Quoyle the boat. That was all that was left of him. But he more or less set the story going.

For a long time I'd wanted to write about a newspaperman anyway, and it seemed that in order to tell this story about Newfoundland—and I wanted to tell it through an American—the only way, the only occupation I could think of that would convincingly allow me to put an American in this place where there were absolutely no jobs at all, was to put him in a newspaper situation. Of course, a newspaper is a perfectly fabulous vehicle for describing the social structure of a place and time; witness what John Dos Passos did in *U.S.A.* So that's more or less the approach.

In Heart Songs, *what came across most strongly to me was the book's deep rooting in Vermont. That was your place. But you've been greatly expanding your territory with each new book. Do you think of yourself as a regional writer, or do you want to go out there and do the whole world?*

I have made a conscious effort not to get tagged "regional writer." There are great regional writers—fine, extraordinary regional writers—and there are also many fine writers who are trapped under the banner, or the rubber hood, of being a

Interview: E. ANNIE PROULX

regional writer. And I think it limits one. I think people who write a first book about a particular place and are identified as regional writers begin to believe indeed that they are regional writers, that that is their territory and they dare not step out of it. It's what they know and they shouldn't go any farther. But I'm very easily bored, and I figured I'd done all I wanted to do with that particular rural setting with *Heart Songs*. So there was a conscious effort on my part not to be a regional writer—unless I wanted to be.

You've said that it was a great relief to you to come to novel writing after short stories because there was more room to move around in them. Does that still hold true?

Short stories—and I thought I was a short-story writer for ten years—were always immensely difficult for me. I mean really, really difficult: draft after draft after draft, and I couldn't get it right, and editors would always complain: "You don't need all this stuff in here; there's too much. You don't need to tell all this about these characters and what they're wearing." And yet I wanted to. I thought it was important. And it never dawned on me that I might be better off writing a novel. It never occurred to me! I hadn't a clue that I might write a novel some day.

So, what about Postcards? *How did that come about?*

A fluke of luck. Here we go with some publishing history: I used to write these short stories, two a year, maybe, when I was cooking, or sometimes three. And I sent them off, and a number of them did get published. *Esquire* did three of them, and Rust Hills, the *Esquire* fiction editor, had an assistant named Tom Jenks who's now the fiction guy for *GQ*—none of those guys seemed to stay there for more than a year or two. Tom Jenks then went on to Scribner's, and called one day and said, "How about we do a collection of your short stories? You've got enough of them, I think."

And I said, "Sure, of course."

So, I bundled up a number of short stories and finished up

She's "from away," but she got it right.

some. It took me a few months to get it all together and send it off, and by that time, Tom Jenks was no longer with Scribner's. This is, you know, modern publishing. And in came John Glusman, now senior editor at Farrar, Straus, Giroux: a marvelous editor. So John was my editor in getting these short stories ready for publication. They were published and got quite good reviews, the collection did. It was okay. But way back, when the option clause in my contract was being drawn up, Tom Jenks had said, "Why don't we just put in 'novel'? You really should think about writing a novel some day."

"Ha, ha," said I, "what a joke. But if it makes you feel better, go ahead, put in 'novel.'"

So he put in "novel" and some low figure, and I promptly forgot about it. I thought some day I might actually work up to doing a second collection of short stories—in another ten years or whenever. But one day John Glusman called, after the short stories had been published and out there a while, and said, "You know, you really ought to think about writing that novel."

"Novel? What novel is that?"

"It says 'novel' in your contract."

It didn't have a name. It was just "a work known as 'Novel.'"

So I sat down at the table and, in half an hour, I had the whole thing for *Postcards* clearly in mind. And it was a great relief to have room. It was wonderful!

In The Shipping News, *there are a number of narrative threads that are woven together extraordinarily well, whereas* Postcards *has a more improvisatory feel. Was* The Shipping News *the more meticulously planned book?*

In both cases, it was deliberate. Because *Postcards* is a road book and because Loyal was a character who wandered at random, I wanted that spacy, random, stumbled-across, maybe-it-happened-maybe-it-didn't feeling in it. That was deliberate. I worked hard to get that effect with *Postcards*.

In *The Shipping News,* because of the knot theme, I literally

Interview: E. ANNIE PROULX

wanted to braid together ropes of story. So this is a game for me. I like to have a little puzzle or game in everything I write. I had these little threads and strung them through the whole thing, and tried to come out with some kind of a knot at the end: a stopper knot. And it was great fun to do, to try to pull this off. I had much private amusement working with these thin little bits of stories through the whole thing.

Have you kept up with friends or acquaintances you made in Newfoundland?

God, yeah. When we were talking about the details of things, I was going to tell you this story about a couple who came down to visit. *This* detail never would have occurred to me. I haven't written it down anywhere, but it's a great story to tell. This couple lives up on the Great Northern Peninsula, at the far end where the only trees are low-growing tuckamore, no trees higher than your waist; it's all bare rock. They came down two falls ago and stayed at the house when the leaves were at their height, and the day they came we had a big hugging and squeezing and so forth. It was nighttime and we ate a big dinner and all that. And the next morning they went out onto the deck, or the wife went out onto the deck. She came back in with her eyes on stalks and she says to her husband, "Come out 'ere!"

"What is it?"

So he goes out there, and they're talking excitedly, and I thought, What the hell is it? Maybe they're seeing deer up on the hillside. They have moose in Newfoundland, but not much else. And I went out there, and they turned to me with this expression of ecstatic surprise on their faces and they said, "They makes noise!"

"What makes noise?"

"Leaves! The leaves is making noise!"

You know? The wind blowing through the leaves? They had never heard that. Here are two adults who had never heard wind blowing through leaves. And that's the kind of thing you want

She's "from away," but she got it right.

to watch for. You've got to find these things out. There's nothing like a fresh eye—and that's my best example of a fresh eye in a place. No one who lives in New England would have noticed wind in the leaves ever, ever, ever. It took someone from away to see it: the value of the outsider's eye.

Where is Killick-Claw? I kept looking for it in my atlas.

All those places are invented, except for St. John's.

Are all the invented places up on the Northern Peninsula somewhere?

That story is pretty much restricted to the Northern Peninsula, but they're not real places. The real places have much better names. A lot of the rocks, the named rocks in the novel, are real. I came upon a copy of sailing directions for 1861 that listed some of the older rocks around the island, and compared it with the 1990 edition of navigation direction. But the 1861 sailing directory was just a piece of work, with these rich, extraordinary names. Very fun. Very amusing.

What about the sex abuse that gets reported in the Gammy Bird *[the Newfoundland newspaper where Quoyle works]? The amount of it is just mind-boggling. Is that even remotely based on any reality? Or is it total fancifulness on your part?*

No, no, no, no, no. This was the period when the Mount Cashel Orphanage in St. John's had been front-page news for a year and a half, two years, and the trials were just beginning when I started doing this book. And all these scandals, these sex scandals, were part of *all* newspapers in Canada, not just in Newfoundland.

This was the time in the late 1980s, early 1990s, when papers in North America began to print stories about sexual abuse. It seems like a long time ago now, but it really wasn't. It was just a few years ago. Before then, people didn't print things like that in the paper. And then it began in the States, stories, say, about some town somewhere where eleven thousand people were abused out of a population of eighteen thousand. Very much in the news in that period, so that absolutely fits the time.

Interview: E. ANNIE PROULX

A more frivolous question: Why all the ancient Ontario phone books? [In the book, Quoyle keeps noticing Ontario phone directories, dating from as long ago as the 1960s.]

As it happens, I have a good answer for that. This is one of those little running details in the book that I really like to put in. Newfoundland has been in economic trouble for a long time. There are no jobs there. Anybody who wants to make a living doing anything but fishing—and now anybody who wants to make a living *including* fishing—has to go somewhere else, i.e., to the mainland. And where are all the jobs on the mainland? Where's the big hub? Ontario. So you go to Ontario and you look for a job and you don't find one and you come back home. And what do you bring with you, just in case? You bring the Ontario telephone directory. So, all over Newfoundland, you find these old Ontario telephone directories that are like little signs of hope that some day a job will be gotten on the mainland and all of those dreams of television sets and fancy cars and beefsteaks, and so forth, will come true. The crucial element is the Ontario telephone directory.

During the period you're drawing on for The Shipping News, *the fishing situation sounds bad. But I assume that it must have gone to yet another degree of desperation just in this past year.*

If you've been following the news, you know it's exceedingly serious. The manuscript was finished about three or four months before the fishing moratorium came down several years ago. The Canadian government decided, belatedly, that it would be a good idea if nobody went fishing for cod in order to let the cod stock recover. And so this moratorium came down. Fishermen were paid either a lump sum—if they swore they'd get out of fishing forever, the "package"—or unemployment insurance. I don't really know the exact details of it, but there was some kind of a stipend to keep them going while the cod stock recovered.

Well, I was up there in January, doing a special on *The Shipping News* for the CBC program *Prime Time News,* and the story

She's "from away," but she got it right.

broke: The Canadian biologists, the fisheries' biologists who were tracking the cod stock, came in with their report. This was at the end of January '94, and the report was the most awful news that anybody could imagine. Completely unexpected. They said that not only had the cod stock *not* recovered, but it also had plunged to some incredibly low percentage of what it was when the moratorium was first put on. It was something like five percent of what it had been two years ago.

They said that the cod stock, the northern cod, were on the verge of extinction. Not just at low numbers, but at unprecedentedly low numbers, at frighteningly low numbers. One of the great food supplies of the world, thought to be inexhaustible at one time! So thick were the cod in the North Atlantic that ships literally had difficulty making their way through them. Now there weren't any left. And the reasons? Global warming apparently has something to do with it, because the Greenland glaciers are calving icebergs with greater and more formidable frequency than ever—so that all of these waters are now just chockablock with ice. And the ice has chilled down the waters so much that the cod are not breeding in their traditional spot. They've moved somewhat to the south.

Alas, where they've chosen to go is off the nose and the tail of the Grand Banks. The Grand Banks falls within the two-hundred-mile limit of Canadian territory. But the nose and the tail—this little bit that sticks out on two ends—do not. They're just outside the two-hundred-mile limit, i.e., where all the foreign draggers and trawlers are parked, scooping everything up. All of this, of course, affected by years and years of the Canadian government letting foreigners fish in return for one favor or another: total mismanagement of the fishing stock, and then trying to mend it later. What we have is a hideous concatenation of events that nobody could have foreseen, that is literally destroying the old outport life. There is nothing left there for fishermen, as people have been for hundreds of years.

Interview: E. ANNIE PROULX

What about oil? [Oil is mentioned as a possible source of jobs and revenue in the novel.] What's happening with that?
Nothing. That was down off St. John's. There is still much talk, and so forth. That's definitely not a solution for the outports, which are hundreds of miles away from there, anyway, and not many people would be employed in that. So, there we are. Those little outports on the Northern Peninsula depended a hundred percent on the fisheries for their livelihood.

One old guy said to me, "What am I gonna do? What am I gonna do? I'm not trained for anything. You think they're gonna give me a job? Look at me!" he says. "All I can do is fish! It's all I know."

We have a similar situation here with the logging industry, where they've overforested. The same thing goes on.

Let me ask you a little bit about your writing style. I noticed in reading Heart Songs *and* The Shipping News *side by side that there's quite a difference between the two. The Shipping News is more experimental, with a lot of compression in the prose. And yet the effect is a kind of crystallization, so that it's actually more lucid, easier to read: sharp words that enter the mind directly with a minimum of syntactical structure around them. I wondered how deliberate that was?*

What I was trying to do there—and I *was* trying to do something—was a failure in one sense. But it worked in another way. You may have seen the old newspapers that used to have a lot of subheads. Each story had these subheads that were just tiny, compressed *précis* of what the story was about, one after another. I thought that if I cast my sentences in "subheadese" it would give a newspapery flavor to the whole book. So that's what I had in mind when I went to that very terse, truncated kind of style. But it didn't work that way.

How it worked was as an interiorization of Quoyle's thoughts and actions. So it *did* work, but not quite as I had intended. I'm not displeased with it because we often talk that way, in bits and pieces and chunks of sentences, with much left out. So it had a

She's "from away," but she got it right.

flavor of conversation or immediacy to it, too, which was okay for that particular story.

The style and the sentence structure, the rhythm, the balance—all these things I take a lot of trouble with—must suit the story. To find a style that's just right for the story you're doing takes some experimentation and fooling around. I did try writing *The Shipping News,* a chapter or two, with longer sentences and just didn't like it as much. It was tiresome.

Heart Songs was really experimental. I learned a lot in doing those short stories, and I learned a lot from John Glusman. I learned how to get rid of adjectives and I learned about balance. I learned how important balance is. And I learned how bloody, fucking important *structure* is. If you can't get the structure, stay home, baby.

Was The Shipping News *always a third-person narrative?*

Yeah, I'm very happy with third person. I find writing in first person enormously constraining. It's like having a bloody straitjacket on, and who needs it? I love being able to back up as far as possible and *literally* look at the landscape from a vantage point above, or I love being able to get directly close to the characters and even, in some sense, get inside them.

How about vocabulary? You have quite an unusual vocabulary. I was constantly running to Random House II *to find "gledgy eyes" or "scrob," as in "to scrob and claw through hard times."*

You found "gledgy"?

I didn't!

It's in the unabridged. That's not a Newfoundland word. That's in the unabridged. I use an old *Webster's Unabridged.* I do collect dictionaries, and I do read them, and I do keep word lists, and I do make notes of language. I have big notebooks, page after page of words that I like or find interesting or crackly, or whatever. And from time to time I will also, if I feel a section is a bit limp, take a couple of days and just do dictionary work and recast the sentences so that they have more power because their words aren't overused. And often the search for the right word can consume a lot of time, but usually it can be found. I've put

Interview: E. ANNIE PROULX

a lot of effort into finding the right word instead of using a scattershot approach.
The milk "firping" into the pail in Postcards? *I assumed you were coining some of these, but no?*
No. There are enough words there for me. There really are enough wonderful words to be used. Some of them are not used much, and they ought to be.
I need a new dictionary.
Also, for *The Shipping News,* there was another dictionary that I used that I could not have written the book without, and that is *The Dictionary of Newfoundland English* by George M. Story, W.J. Kirwin, and J.D.A. Widdowson. It's one of the great lexicographical works of our century, an extraordinary dictionary, exceedingly rich.

It's now in its second edition and, unfortunately, Mr. Story, blessed be his name, died only three weeks ago. A professor of English and etymology at Memorial University in St. John's, he was a Newfoundlander who went to Oxford, could have gone anywhere in the world, and came back to Newfoundland where he spent his scholarly life. He's known for many other things besides this, but this is perhaps his most wonderful piece of scholarship. This is the most readable dictionary I've ever held in my hands. Every word is illustrated with sentences, either written examples or overheard, and the dates are given for the occurrences and often the place. It's grand. It's a history, a history of the language, as much as anything else. Most of these words are from Ireland and the west of England originally, and they've remained somewhat pure in parts of Newfoundland, or they've been shifted around. Speak of neologisms, that's where you'll find them. Newfoundlanders make up words to suit the case. Great ones! Like "scruncheons," which are little tiny bits of fried pork, so they're both chewy and hard at the same time. They're delicious little tidbits. So it was fun to give the gossip column in the *Gammy Bird* the name of "Scruncheons."

What about the characters' names? I read that you find them in the phone book. Do you find them all in the phone book? Diddy Shovel?

56   Glimmer Train Stories

She's "from away," but she got it right.

Biscuit Paragon? Aren't some of them inventions?
Yes. No. Phone books are part of the writer's arsenal. I keep notebooks of names and, when I'm working on a book, I want the names to fit the place. If there's one thing I hate, it's a name that's instantly forgettable, and that's because I'm a reader. I spend a lot of time reading and I don't like to lose track of the characters, and if the characters have good names, I remember them.

I will get the names from phone books, bulletin boards, from tourist information, from bibliographies, lists of fishing guides, park attendants. Anybody! Newspaper advertisements. Stories. Not the whole names, mind you, just first or last. If you're ever looking for names, by the way, Chinese historians have the most amazing names of anybody anywhere.

So, what I'll do is take literally hundreds of first names and hundreds of last names, and make lists of them on opposing pages. And then when it comes time and I've got my character from my other notebook—my character's physical description—I go to my name notebook and poke around until I find a first and a last that fit together okay for that character. And there we are.

In all the books, I've noticed a pronounced fondness for having male protagonists, quite often males who are hooked up with pretty hellacious females. With these male characters, you usually show more sympathy than with the women. What's going on there?
The answer is so simple it will make you throw up.

What is it?
I was the oldest of five girls. I grew up in a family of five girls. If there's one thing I know, it's women and girls. And I don't find them interesting to write about. I find men much more interesting, you know? I didn't know any men when I was a kid, except my father. So it's more fun; it's more interesting.

Also, most of my life the things I've liked to do, the fishing and canoeing and tramping around in the country—this was before everybody got into the outdoorsy number—those were activities where there were not many women; it was mostly men. So

Interview: E. ANNIE PROULX

I palled around with guys most of my adult life, and felt more at home with the direct approach to things that was then labeled "masculine." Now you can find women like that, too, and I know a lot of women whom I like a lot. Just great women out there.

Anyway, the two novels both demanded male protagonists. They were not set in a time or a place when those stories could have been written with women. I don't *think* of stories around women. And that's undoubtedly, in these days of political correctness, an enormous flaw in my character. But, baby, that's how it is.

There's a passage in The Shipping News *where Agnis [Quoyle's aunt, who helps him make the move to Newfoundland] describes the "forces of fate" as being "weakened by unemployment insurance." She seems to be registering a sizeable social change, both in Canada and in this country. You've mentioned that your studies of history gave you a sense of how important a writer's sense of underlying social change can be to creating fiction. Are there particular social changes that fascinate you?*

Change itself is what fascinates me. I am drawn, as a moth to the flame, by edge situations, by situations of metamorphosis and change, by things turning from one into another, by those little magic eggs within eggs within eggs, like those Russian dolls. This kind of thing, this shifting and sliding away—the sand moving under one's feet, the tide coming in and changing the look of the coastline—these are the things that pull my eye. And the study of history satisfies that taste, and that *is* why I studied history, and this is why I happen to write books of stories that deal with change, either in an individual life or on a broad social scale.

It's fortunate for me—or unfortunate, depending on your viewpoint—that I did have historical training and do have something of a trained eye to look at social change, and that's always the basis of the books I write, both *Postcards* and *The Shipping News,* and the one I'm working on now, and the ones to come. Maybe it sounds like I'm in a rut, but that's the kind

She's "from away," but she got it right.

of thing that pleases me. And it's not specific social changes that attract me. It's really any social change. I just like seeing the situation where everything seems chaos, and only a little is revealed or resolved. But enough is revealed or resolved to give shape and form to the story. I do not like the pseudo-Chekhovian "trailing away."

Agnis, to my mind, embodies a kind of stoicism and dry humor that gives the book a lively positive thrust. Do you share that stoic and humorous approach to life? Are those your main implements for getting through it?

Oh, perhaps. But what I was trying to do with Agnis was this: In the study of history and in reading diaries and accounts of people's lives, particularly in sociological studies of people from poverty-stricken areas and different ethnic groups that are in poverty-line situations, I was struck—one cannot help but be struck—by the human capacity for endurance. One gets through. One gets through. People do get through, and I wanted a character who was not so much stoic as not going to give up, who would determine to not hang up on the rough stuff, not whine, not go through a twelve-step, but to tough it through and get on the other side. I liked that for Agnis, and a lot of people do that. That's how people get through life. Life is wretched for many people, and it doesn't get better as one gets older, so I just wanted Agnis to be toughing the awful stuff through. That was just her character—it's not me in particular.

There's a point in The Shipping News *where Quoyle is reading the* Gammy Bird *and is startled by how the paper looks at life "right in its shifty, bloodshot eye." Is that your purpose with fiction? Are the* Gammy Bird *and your fiction trying to do the same thing?*

I don't know... The *randomness* of things and the hammer of life is something that intrigues me very much. A lot of vicious, hard, dreadful, evil things happen to people through no fault of their own. The stuff just comes down and hammers them. Life does that, and some people get hammered again and again. And this sense of the inescapability of the hammer, of turning to look at it as it descends on you, is something I do try to catch from time

Interview: E. ANNIE PROULX

to time. It sounds kind of ghastly. You turn and look at the executioner's axe descending, and recognize, at some point, what it is that's happening to you, what you're seeing—that flying thought has occurred to me more than once when that kind of thing happens in the prose. Yes, looking life in its "shifty, bloodshot eye." So, in that sense, you're right.

You've done all kinds of journalism and articles. Have you ever been attracted by travel writing? I notice Quoyle reads books by "Erics Newby and Hansen."

I love reading those.

In all your roaming around, have you thought of writing one yourself? Or what about a book just on the weather? The weather in The Shipping News *is so extraordinary.*

No, everything goes into the fiction. Certainly the fiction can carry all this. It's a basket for all of these interests, and there isn't any other that can tote so many along as fiction—for me, anyway. I really haven't done any travel writing, and I don't think I will. I'll probably put everything into the fiction. I still do some magazine work from time to time, mostly for *Outside,* and I promised some things to *Gourmet,* but it's not a big part of my life.

A phrase in the title story of Heart Songs *caught my eye, when the main character feels a "secret revulsion at the thought of success." Your success has been raining down on your head in a big way this past year, and I wondered—*

I'm not going to answer this question! I see where you're going! No! Okay, sure. At this point all I want is to go back to my little corner with my books and my pen and my pencil and paper, and get back to work. It's been a great ride; I've met some wonderful people, but I wouldn't want to do it every day. It's a great place to visit, but I wouldn't want to live there, in Prize Land.

It's very encouraging to people who are a little slow in getting their fiction off the ground, to see someone hit their stride in their fifties. Did your stories brew for years and years in your head? What change of situation got you going at the particular moment when you did?

She's "from away," but she got it right.

Having the time—and when my publisher gave me an advance and said, "Go write a novel."
So, it was purely economic.
No, time was also part of it. My youngest son left home, and these two things coincided. I had money to live without doing anything else, and I had the time, and so I started writing a novel. Those two things helped a great deal. If you don't have to go out and work at another job, or rob banks, or something like that, it's very, very pleasant. So the stories really did not brood a long time. I have a lot of stories. All my life has been an interest in stories, forever and ever and ever. So finding the stories is not the hard part. Writing them down is.
When did you first know you would be doing fiction?
I was writing fiction when I was a kid, but, you know, not seriously. Every now and then I'd write a story, and then I wouldn't do it for years, and then I'd write another story. Some of them would be published, but I didn't try very hard, didn't actually start doing it seriously until fifteen years ago. Then I knew I really wanted to write fiction at that point. I really *wanted* to, and thought I was a short-story writer. I was so dumb. I hadn't a clue that I could write a novel. I thought novels were for "advanced writers." You had to have some kind of secret ceremony where someone said, "All right, you are now a novelist."
The dust jacket of Heart Songs *mentions earlier nonfiction books. Would they be of interest to people who like your fiction?*
No, no. They were books done on assignment, about making cheese and cider and growing salad gardens, and that kind of thing. They were done strictly for money. That's all. So-and-so calls up and says, "Will you do us a book on potatoes?" And I say, "Yeah."
They were interesting to do, but with no particular merit to them. They're credible and they're decently done, and there *are* footnotes. They're competently written; that's all I can say.
How many of them are there?
Oh, I don't know. Seven or eight, maybe? Once in a while,

Interview: E. ANNIE PROULX

someone displays one and flashes it before my eyes and waits for me to scream with delight and they're always bitterly disappointed when I don't. They were jobs of work, plain and simple. I'm not ashamed of them, but they don't turn me on. Very, very different kind of writing than the fiction.

One last frivolous question: On page 288 of The Shipping News *I suddenly became aware that Quoyle's initials are R.G. when his name appears on the masthead of the* Gammy Bird. *Have I missed his first name somewhere?*

No, no. I just knew it wasn't possible to have on the masthead a managing editor with one name. I couldn't have just Quoyle, so I had to have an R.G. I felt bad about it.

Do you know what his name is?

No. His name is Quoyle. The R.G. was just something I stuck in so it would look better. It's too bad. It destroys the symmetry. But it would have been more of an imbalance to have it read: "Managing Editor: Quoyle." That would have been too much. Let it be R.G.

MICHAEL UPCHURCH is a Seattle writer whose novels include *Air* and *The Flame Forest*.

She's "from away," but she got it right.

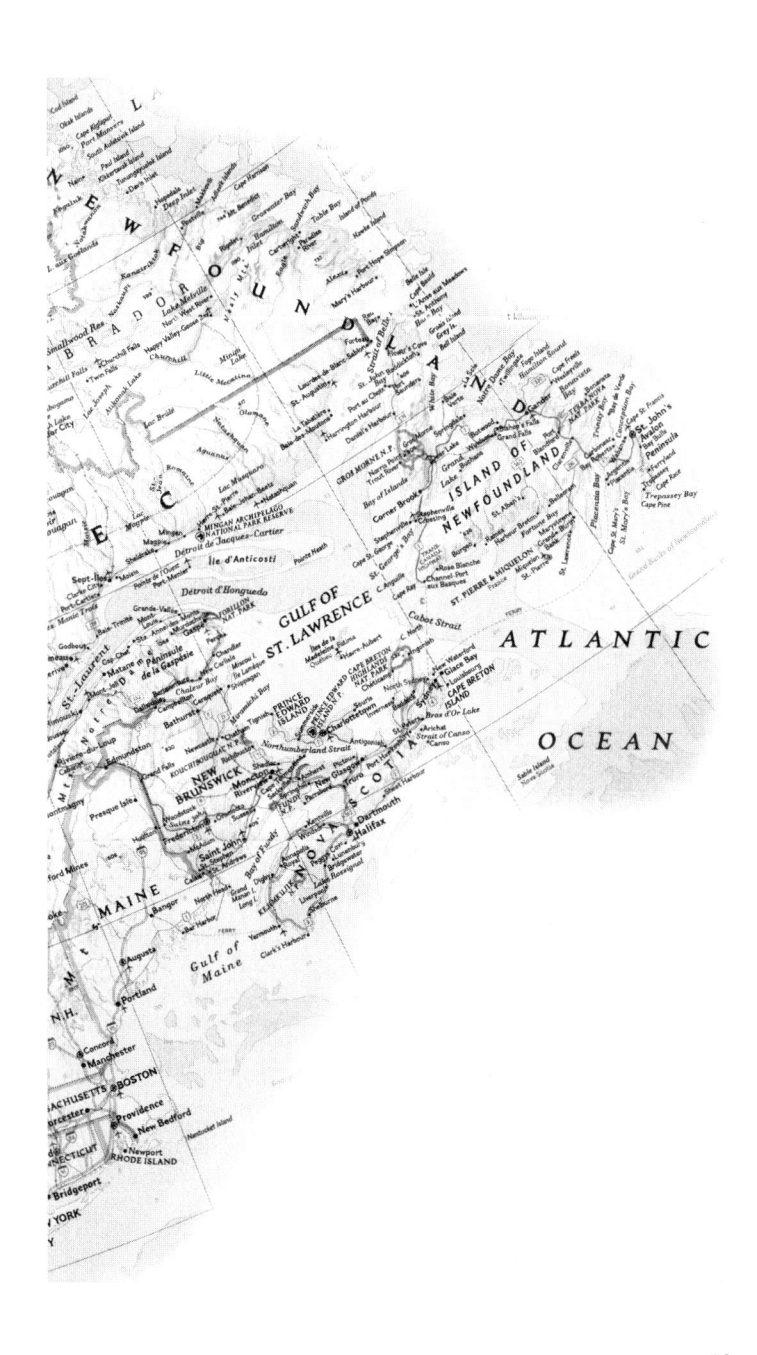

Lara Stapleton

Our father is a statistician, thus the attraction to numbers. Many of our early photographs have our heights and weights included. This was 1973. All three of us have inherited that ability with numbers, but despite my father's noble efforts, have opted for the liberal arts.

Lara Stapleton's stories have been published in the *Michigan Quarterly Review*, the *Alaska Quarterly Review*, the *Asian-Pacific American Journal*, and *Columbia*. She is now completing a collection entitled *One Of*.

Stapleton was born and raised in Michigan. A recent graduate of NYU's creative-writing program, she teaches in the city college system in New York.

LARA STAPLETON
Joselito

*I*f only he wouldn't have to try to be such a man about everything. He is only thirteen, and already he insists on turning the corner before his sister/cousin, on being first into empty subway hallways, on taking the first step into traffic, a hand to the small of her back, like a date. He is so small, a young-looking thirteen, that it makes people laugh. His sister/cousin is ten years older.

Usually, she thinks his machismo is cute. He has to walk in front of every basketball expedition, could be six grown men—six neighbors or cousins and cousins' boyfriends, and he would have to walk in front and in the most exaggerated way. He would talk the most shit. "Yo, Alfie, Ima fuck you up. Yo, yo, yo, yo, Alfie, check this out—Ima fuck you up." His voice is still like a girl's.

Even today while he walks behind, with Julia fuming on up ahead, even with his eye swollen shut like the cleave of a muffin top, Joselito glares at the men on the street who stare at his sister. She's carrying a cane on her shoulder like a bayonet, which makes for easy openings: "Hey Mami, you need some help with that?" "You goin' off to war, Sugar?" "You into, like, domination?" Joselito glares with his good eye, as if Julia wouldn't be better off alone.

Julia's teeth might crack with gritting. She walks full-stride toward the subway. She knows Lito will follow, because Alfie

Lara Stapleton

told him to. Alfie is Julia's boyfriend, the only one Lito listens to. Her cousin has threatened to run away lately, disappeared full days at a time, but today Julia knows he'll follow. She is livid and it shows in her pace.

She said she'd hit him. After the other boy took a swing and Lito scrambled and cursed, Julia said, "Joselito, if you do not come home with me right now, I am going to smack you right here. I do not care how many black eyes you got." She said it loud enough for everyone. Julia knows Lito would never hit a girl, at least not in public. The most infuriating thing, though, was that it took Alfie, that Alfie had to take the kid roughly by the chin and look in the open eye and say, "Go home with your sister right now."

Someone says, "Oh shit, Baby. I feel sorry for that mufucka when you catch up with him." And then sees her brother and says, "Oh, I guess you already caught up."

Lito's skin feels shaved by cement, stings all over. They're marching toward the E train, Julia muttering. Joselito is a little ashamed but mostly feeling cool. His blue Gap T-shirt is bloody down the front. Monday at school, they'll know he means business. The people staring as they pass must know Lito defended his sister. He is a force to be reckoned with. Monday, he'll tell how somebody was calling his sister something on the street.

Julia bursts, "What if we weren't there? Huh? What then? What happens when me and Alf are not there to save your ass every time you open your stupid mouth?"

"I can take care of myself." His bottom lip juts. He's cringing.

"Bullshit." Julia throttles him with her empty hand. His eyeball feels loose and bouncing as she shakes. Her fingers pinch his elbow. He is tender and sore all over.

There was a friendly stranger in the park for a game of pickup. He was older, a young uncle's age instead of an older brother's like the rest of the guys. He said to Alfredo, "Man, you better

Joselito

tell that kid to slow down. Somebody'll take him a little too seriously one day soon..."

One day soon was an hour later in the second game when a kid who was big for thirteen asked what the fuck his problem was. Lito never knew when the joke turned serious. One second, everyone was laughing; next, it felt like his eye would pop to the inside of his skull.

He has to fill up space. If you don't make noise and fill it, then someone else might.

Lito is crying quietly out of his good eye; the bad runs a little pus. He is kind of old not to have learned how not to cry. Everything is blurry. He is more volatile this way. Things take on a delicacy as they pass. Everything that's breakable looks breakable, everything bendable calling for dents. Buildings and cars and especially bus stops have windows. Trash cans and street signs might bend over sideways. Anyone could knock over a shuffling old man with one hand, or rip the baby from a young mother's arms, kick a stroller right into the street. These are things that could happen at any moment and only happen once in a while.

Julia is glad she's got the cane. It's a smooth yellow piece of wood with a little green band, like a pool cue with a handle. She grabbed it instinctively as the yelling got louder. She considers cracking it on the curb.

He got the cane from an MTV video. Some of the kids are using them to dance with and some of the kids are using them all the time just for style. "Don't you know that cane makes people want to start with you?" Julia said.

One time, somebody asked, "Use that cane instead of a dick?"

"Shut the fuck up, man," Lito answered in his girl's voice. Julia put herself in the middle that time, too. Most don't really want to fight, and a girl in the middle is a good reason to call the whole thing off.

She said, "Half the city with guns and you got this stick like it makes you a man."

But Lito controls the delicacy with the cane. With the cane, the windows don't shatter because he chooses not to shatter them. Old ladies hobbling are an act of his kindness.

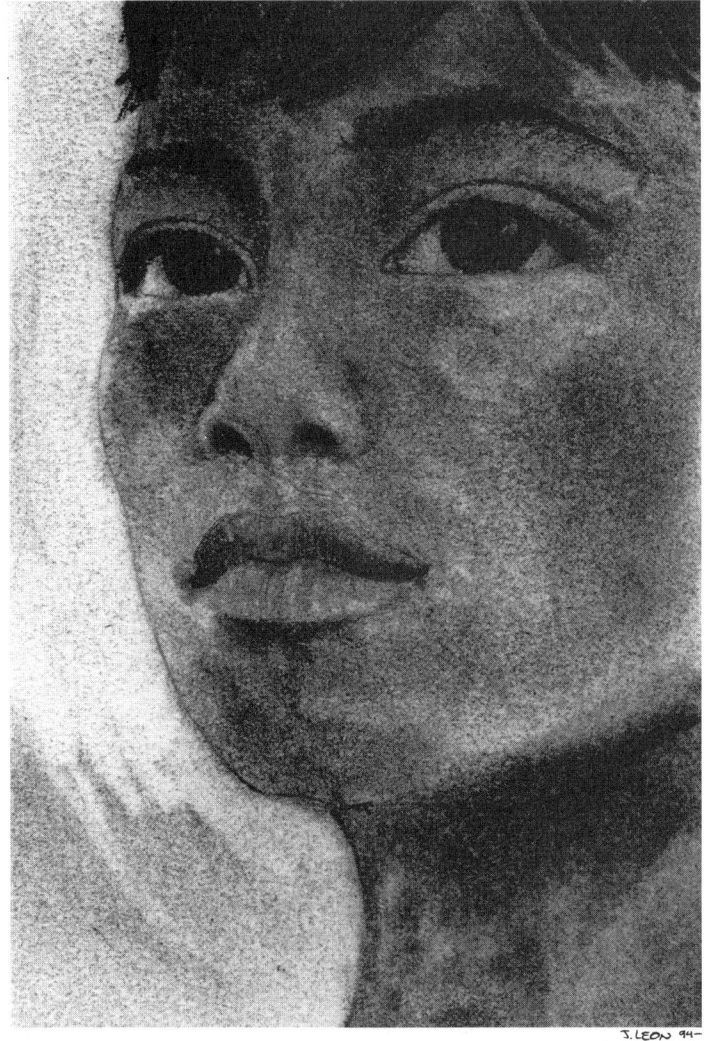

His aunt/mother, Perla, thinks the cane is the last straw. "I will not have my child behaving like a hoodlum." She has handed

Joselito

two to Julia already and asked her to break them on the stoop. The third was confiscated at school. The fourth he hides on the bottom rung of the fire escape.

"Ma, it's just a trend," says Julia. "Remember when he had to have those shoes that puff up?"

"Yes, those puff-up shoes," says Perla.

"It's the same thing. It's just fashion, Ma. Just something all the kids do. He just has to be trendy. That's all. Ma, he gets some Bs. He's okay."

Perla is not convinced.

Before the cane, his prop was a basketball. That was a good prop for a kid to have. He had one tucked under his arm for a solid year and a half, fifth and sixth grade. He played almost every day after school and, on Saturdays, Julia's boyfriend would take him.

That is Lito's favorite thing about his own life—Julia's boyfriend. Alf calls Lito "Flyboy" for his sideways hat. Julia, and even Perla, call him Flyboy sometimes now, only when Perla says it, it sounds like Plyboy, so now Alfie says "Plywood," too. Alfie was the first time Julia introduced Lito as her brother instead of her cousin. He'd been with them three years and she'd figured it was time. He lit up when she said it so it became the truth. Lito likes it when Alfie tells him what to do.

"Sit back and shut up, Flyboy, so we can all enjoy the movie, okay?"

"All right, all right." Lito would fake-mope on top. Underneath, he'd be beaming. With Alfie, Lito will turn back to follow girls, knowing he'll be grabbed by the scruff of the neck. He'll hover by the subway gate, waiting for Alf to say, "Get back and pay the fare."

Julia drops two tokens in the turnstile, not bothering to see if Joselito has his own. He leans his head against a pillar. Julia's face is just like the token-booth lady's, fed up. Not even mad

LARA STAPLETON

anymore. Sisters and mothers are scarier beyond mad; that's when they decide to change things.

"Can I have my cane?" He's whispering, speaking down at his bloody Gap T-shirt. He feels small, wants to hold something. "Please?"

"No way."

He wishes she would touch him. He is reaching for that inside part, a button to turn off.

Before the basketball, Lito's prop was a pillow. It was an armrest pillow, a gray-blue tube off the couch he stole into his bedroom. Perla would find it in the mornings wet with saliva. He nuzzled it. He pressed his tiny nose without cartilage against the pillow. This was when he first came, when all they could do was marvel at his prettiness and hope he'd get happy again. His little nose like two holes in his face, lips always wet. His color was so bright, a warm yellow-brown, warm like toast or a stream of sun through the window.

Joselito does not mean Little José in Tagalog, as it meant to the Spanish. It just means Joselito. It says Joselito on the birth certificate. Lito is usually the nickname, and he'll never become José. He was born in Manila and everything was fine for a while. He had a mother who was not an aunt and a father and a baby brother and a collection of Japanese robots he buzzed sound effects for. He went to school. He was good at futbol and singing. But reading was quick and slippery, an eel. Just when he thought he had it, all the rules would change and be gone. How did everyone else get it when the rules changed all the time? Even when he thought he had it, when he had one hand tight around the base of the neck, the other halfway down, he'd bring his prize to his teacher and be told he was wrong.

He was nine, and got D after D and then an F, until his papa, his chubby Filipino father, Papa, whose face is blurry now, would sit him at the kitchen table with his books for two hours

Joselito

every night. After dinner, an alarm clock would tick down his sentence. He stared at the books. The ink pulsed and writhed until he forgot the black part meant more than the shapes the white made around it. And his penmanship—the blue lines jumped over and under his letters. As soon as he memorized right and left, the sides got switched, along with the rules about angles and hoops, lines up and down, lines across.

After a time, instead of staring at the twitching little inkballs, he might stare at lamps until he could close his eyes and see splotches on his lids, as vivid as cartoons. He might see insects, or *Mazinga-Zee*, the Japanese spaceship shaped like a soldier. He might make up a song, tiny rhythms with his fingers on the table, or when his father looked up to see him goofing off, he might make it more secret by scrunching up rhythms with his toes. He decided there were other things to make up for being stupid, like being good at futbol or girls thinking you are cute. But these are things you cannot tell your parents. All they want is for you to stop being stupid and they spank you and take your robots and sit you at the table with the squirmy ink. It gets so something cold trickles whenever you see a book. One day you can't get out of bed and then it's too hot for school, too hot to sit up and vomit. Mama asked why he didn't use the bucket and Lito was too weak to explain *Mazinga-Zee* came in his sleep to say it was okay to vomit on the sheets. Someone else would clean it up. There were doctors and more doctors and finally someone said there are even more doctors who can fix dumbness. The only problem is that they are on the other side of the world. Lito's parents would want a smart son so they'd be glad to get rid of him.

Everything might burn. If, one day, your parents couldn't take it and they packed you off, screaming, into an airplane, maybe they were lying that it would land at your aunt's house and that your aunt looked just like your mother and would be just as

LARA STAPLETON

good to you. They might be lying, because they said the plane wouldn't hurt, but as soon as it got in the air, a shrill alarm went off in his head. His head was pumping up like a balloon that might pop and who knows what might happen since your mother might stop loving you one day. And who knows if you'll make it to the bathroom or if you're even allowed to leave the seat, so you might as well wait here in the first seat before the seats get bigger, where the blonde lady tied you down. You might as well wait here and cup it in your hand and feel the pressure in two places until one or the other explodes and you have no clothes in the one bag, just comic books and a robot, so you have to wear a towel. You are nine years old, a grown boy who cannot read and everyone is staring at you and laughing and angry. They are so angry they wake up looking for who to blame. You make them sit in stink like poor people.

What he remembers most is the air. How a place could be so different right down to the taste of the air. It was dry and dusty in New York, like you might choke, flammable. It smelled like the wrong gust of wind could knock a cigarette butt into the dry, dry wood of the dry, dry air.

He said to other kids, "Would you accompany me to da canteen?" He bolted to his feet before teachers, said "Yes, Mum." In four months his accent was gone.

The E train comes, and Julia pulls Lito on by the elbow. She points where he should sit and then takes a seat a good five feet from him. Lito's eye is maroon, throbbing. Alfie had joked, "No difference, Plywood, your eye was squinty anyways."

It might look like she hit him, especially with the cane on her lap, so Julia hands the stick over. Lito holds it between his knees. What a sight—the eye, the cane, and bloody Gap T-shirt. They pull out; everyone's pupils twitch off the pillars until the windows are black and the passengers look back at each other.

Joselito

Eventually, he learned tricks. Things help. A hat and sneakers feel better than old-fashioned school shoes, penny loafers. A knapsack, a basketball, a cane, anything to touch so you don't have to worry about where to put your hands. Things make you feel strong. And he learned what to think. If you think hard—do long division or make mental lists of the last ten movies you saw or top five girls you'd like to kiss—you are thinking too hard to look worried. They can be a few years older and twice as big, and you will not look self-conscious, and you might not even hear them, if you are trying hard to list meals for the last four days or every teacher you ever had.

Perla wants to send him back. He can read now, pretty well. The specialist said that it was not severe and he has learned to unscramble, approximate, do the best he can. He still writes poorly, but that can be explained.

Julia said about his disappearing, about suspension, "Ma, it's no big deal," and her mother was not convinced. She said, "Ma, what if we moved to Long Island?" They have moved twice already in Queens.

Perla said, "Julia, he is my sister's child. I am not his mother."

Julia called her mother cruel and Perla smacked her.

At Times Square, a dark-black woman boards with her light-skinned daughter. They look just alike except for their color. The girl has hazel eyes and long curly hair. The woman wears thick chin-length braids that look like they'd tickle. There is no reason for them to stand. There are four or five places they both could sit, ten if the woman would put the girl on her lap.

"Pick me up. Pick me up," says the child. She is kindergarten age. Her arms stretch up.

"Oh, my love, I spoil you," says Mother, lifting her onto her hip, leaning against the closed door. Her accent speaks faintly of the Caribbean—Jamaica, Virgin Islands. Something about her would make you think of flower petals, the shape of her eyes, the velvety plum complexion.

"I want lipstick," says the child, her fingers wide on the end of her little straight arm.

"No lipstick, my love. Not until you are a teenager." Mama's got candy-colored lips. She's smiling. The girl plants a kiss quickly and comes off with half a mouth of bright red and a spiel of giggles. Joselito watches. His ribs go warm.

"Naughty girl," says the woman, rubbing off the color with a thumb. The daughter struggles to kiss her again, squirms to press her face to the mother's. Mama turns her head from side to side and gets it on the ear, the neck, the cheek.

The girl shrieks with joy. No one is looking at Lito and Julia anymore. The people on the train are watching the little girl. Mama covers her mouth with her hand and gets pecks all over her wrist. She pulls her lips in against her teeth. "I tol' you no liptick," she says, like an old lady missing dentures, and gets it all over her mouth without lips.

Lito took to calling everybody "niggahs." Blacks, Filipinos, Puerto Ricans, East Indians, whites—everyone he knows, including dogs panting next to their owners. "Yo, check out this niggah with the stupid fat furry coat." "Look at that dumb niggah." "Ima drop that niggah." "That niggah is bugged." "That niggah is a trip." "I'd be one dead niggah..."

Perla said, "I will not have you speak such things in my house."

"Oh Tita. It don't mean nothin'."

"Anything. It does not mean anything. Listen to you with your accent, and I speak English better than you. Joselito, you forget, we are Filipinos."

Lito's eyebrows pulled tight to the center. "Tita, what is that supposed to mean? What is that supposed to mean?"

Julia thinks how if he gets sent back, he'll be like dead to them.

Joselito

She has never been to the Philippines.

Before Queens Plaza, the train slows down and the passengers' eyes vibrate off the pillars again. The woman with the girl turns to exit. She sets the child down, takes her hand curled over one long pointer finger. The doors separate and then the girl sees something shiny and silver on the floor and reaches down for it. It might be the lipstick tube, but it's a quarter and the doors shut. The mother is on the other side and they are moving. The girl loses balance and lands on her little behind.

There are a lot of things you might do. You could pull the emergency alarm or run right to the conductor and tell him what happened so they can fix it at the next stop, make an announcement. You can hold onto the girl at the next station and make sure she doesn't get even more lost, try to quiet her screaming, ask her her name, tell her everything is gonna be okay. If you're fast enough, you can make a motion out the window to the woman that you'll be at the next stop waiting with the hysterical child.

These things jump in the heads of everyone looking. Split seconds. But it's just Lito who stands, his cane a thud to the floor, the only one in the car on his feet, taking steps, moving without knowing what he'll do when he gets there. In those seconds, the train stops. The mother must have flagged the conductor. He is a man with his head out the window who gets tired of people's curses as they're just a few steps short. You gotta close the doors sometime, but he knows panic and a young mother when he sees it. So the doors open and the young mother grabs her girl, hugs her with a gasp, spanks her. Lito quietly picks up his cane and sits down a little closer to his sister/cousin, who, in a way he can't put his finger on, is moving farther away.

Pete Fromm

With my twin brother, Paul (on the right), beginning an adventurous streak that hasn't seemed to slow yet, for either one of us, though there have been occasional setbacks, such as the one pictured.

Pete Fromm is the author of two story collections, *The Tall Uncut* and *King of the Mountain*, the novel *Monkey Tag*, and the autobiographical *Indian Creek Chronicles*, which won the Pacific Northwest Booksellers Award in 1994. "Helmets" is from a just-completed collection, *Dutch Elm*.

Fromm lives in Great Falls, Montana, and is currently working on a new novel, *Under the Bear's Paw*.

PETE FROMM
Helmets

As our buses rushed into the desert I sat alone in my seat, nearly lulled to sleep by the endless flitting of the sagebrush and the mingling conversations of the other engineers. The sun had just begun to rise at our backs when suddenly, apparently out of nowhere, the Helmet family appeared.

I didn't sit up any straighter at first—a car, after all, while rare this far out, is not unheard of. But as it passed, going the opposite direction, toward town, I caught a glimpse inside. And what I saw was a family: father behind the wheel, mother at the other door, son and daughter occupying the rear seat. Tediously normal, if it were not for the fact that everyone in this family wore helmets. Not steel military issue, but flashy white things. Most likely, nothing more substantial than bicycle helmets. I did sit up straighter then, turning to stare, though, by then, the car was already long gone.

For a moment, I simply gazed at the empty road. Then I glanced around the bus for someone I might tell about what I'd seen. But, with my coworkers an entire generation younger than myself, I rarely spoke on those long rides. So I settled back into my seat, making a mental note to tell Nancy about this strange

PETE FROMM

family that evening during dinner. What in the world did they think they could protect themselves from?

After arriving at the facility, a small crisis in the magnetic containment project kept our team in meetings most of the day. I sat quietly through all of them, wishing I'd been left to work alone at my computer, never being quick enough to think of much to add to these lightning brainstormings. There was a great worry over the possibility of unwanted detonations, but, since my earliest days with DOE, we'd had a nearly unblemished safety record and I wasn't able to muster the same concern as the young men around me. These things always worked out. Instead of listening, I found myself wondering about that family and their helmets, nearly smiling as I imagined how an unwanted detonation would certainly ruin their safe day.

When the meetings finally wrapped up, the team broke into its usual groups, leaving me to get back to my workstation. I'd just flipped on my monitor when my supervisor, Mr. Becker, a thick-haired man half my age, blocked the exit to my cubicle. He smiled and asked if I'd had a chance over the weekend to consider our talk about early retirement.

Glancing at the monitor's cool blue, I slipped my hands beneath my legs. "Nancy and I discussed it, of course," I began, but I couldn't think of another word. Picking at the sturdy weave of the upholstery beneath my fingers, I started over. "Perhaps after ironing out some of this magnetic containment..."

But Mr. Becker interrupted, assuring me my work had been invaluable, but adding, with a small laugh, that he thought they'd be able to muddle on—although, of course, I'd be sorely missed.

With a light slap on my shoulder, a habit of his I could barely stand, he asked me again to give it some serious thought. Before I knew it we were all hustling out to the buses for our sixty-mile ride back to civilization.

Helmets

I picked at my dinner that night, Nancy waiting patiently to hear what was bothering me. She knows I'm not allowed to discuss my projects and, at times, that has been more helpful than I'd care to admit. But tonight she kept waiting, and finally, setting my silverware aside, I said, "Do you remember, Nancy, how exciting everything was when I first started?" Naturally, I'd been thinking a lot about those early days, when even the hush-hush nature of the work seemed to add a flair my life had never known.

"Of course," Nancy said, smiling. "Phyllis threw us the bon voyage party. As if Idaho were in another country."

"Public Relations has replaced the boundary signs again," I said. "INEL this time. Idaho National Engineering Laboratory."

Nancy's smile began to falter, but I continued. "Much less threatening than the Department of Energy Test Site, I suppose. But they've left up the military's 'No Trespassing' signs, and the 'Unexploded Ordnance Area' notices. Who do you suppose they think they're fooling?"

Nancy didn't answer, and I said, "Do you remember when Congress gave us all the money we could ask for? When people still thought we were doing something essential? When it wasn't something to try to hide, to be embarrassed about?"

I realized I'd raised my voice, but Nancy's eyes met mine.

"Those were the exciting years," she agreed, "when everything was so dangerous." But then, lowering her voice to a whisper, she added, "We made a world so dangerous we wouldn't even risk bringing children into it."

When I didn't answer, Nancy quietly raised her plate, asking for more.

"I don't know what's the matter with this country anymore," I muttered, but I forked a thin slice of ham onto Nancy's plate.

It wasn't until I saw the same family the very next day, again helmeted against the world, that I realized I'd forgotten to tell Nancy about them. I reminded myself all day long and, that evening, as soon as we were settled in for dinner, I said to Nancy, "I've seen the oddest thing the past two mornings."

Nancy raised an eyebrow.

I filled her plate and passed it to her. "A family," I continued, "in a car. Coming to town as I go to work."

She listened quietly, a smile waiting to start at the corners of her mouth.

"Every one of them—" I said, pausing, letting the suspense build as I served myself, "mother, father, son, daughter—every one wears a helmet. Every day."

"Helmets?" Nancy asked, her smile breaking across her face, sure she was being teased.

"Helmets!"

"What in heavens for?"

I shrugged hugely. "They must believe it offers them some sort of extra protection. Something the rest of us don't have." My eyes widened in disbelief, accenting the mockery in my voice.

"You can't be serious, Wilton."

"I am, though," I said, smiling myself as I picked up my fork. "Can you believe the naiveté of some people? Why, with even our oldest projects, we could leave nothing of them but white shadows on the road! Helmets!"

Nancy looked at me then, her fingers picking at an ironed wrinkle on the tablecloth, her mouth for a moment as tight as the line in the material. She dipped her head to her dinner and when she looked back up she said they'd started a new program at the grade school where she volunteered. "The MAN project," she said it was called. "Men Are Nice. Some of those children have never known a man who's done anything but abuse them or their mother." She looked at me, shaking her head. "We're looking for men to read stories to them after school. Men just to be kind."

I nodded, but the change of subject wasn't lost on me. Nancy has never liked me talking about my work.

Helmets

The family was there again the next morning, and the next, so regularly I ceased to be surprised by their appearance. In fact, I sat in my seat in the INEL bus and waited for them, tense until their little white sedan rolled past, their helmets flashing white inside. Only then did I ease back into my seat to begin pondering the day's tasks.

This went on for an entire week before I realized the family had begun to interrupt my thoughts even while I worked. I would find myself suddenly woken as if from a trance, staring into some unfinished design on my monitor, realizing I had only been wondering about that family and their silly helmets. Often I would have no idea how much time had been lost.

While perhaps I was never the department's most brilliant design engineer, I was always steady and I was frightened to find myself so easily distracted. The collapse of the cold war undoubtedly sapped some urgency, but even last month, though deeply shaken after first being interrogated about my interest in early retirement, an interest which is absolutely nonexistent, I was back on task within minutes.

The following morning, I listened to the young engineers discuss the newest round of layoffs until I saw the car rolling carefully toward us. As it hugged the shoulder, anticipating our line of buses streaking by, my mind suddenly filled with all the things we could do to their car and their preposterous notions of safety. The stark white outlines left by a nuclear flash weren't even necessary. We had the technology now to blow them into the air first, then atomize them, leaving not a trace of their vain hopes.

As soon as the car swooshed by, however, these thoughts left me quite shaken. I rarely allow myself to dwell upon the use of our work, particularly not in any way so personal or inappropriate. I decided I would have to track down the Helmet family, as Nancy had begun to call them, to see exactly what it was that they thought they could keep so safe.

Pete Fromm

The very next morning, I purposely missed my bus. Feigning annoyance for Nancy's sake, I scrambled into our car and raced out for the desert, hoping to find a spot to wait until I could follow the Helmet family to wherever it was they went. For the first time ever, I fabricated an excuse to explain my absence from work.

I'd just gotten turned around when the white sedan came over the hill, right on schedule, moving completely into the other lane as they went around me, as if I might fling open my door and step blindly into their path—completely unaware of the concept of safety. I pulled out and followed them into Idaho Falls.

The trailing was more difficult in town with the stoplights and traffic. My heart was pounding from a wild acceleration through a mostly yellow light when the white sedan first pulled over. They were in front of a school and I had to stop in the bus area. I watched as the daughter, probably no more than ten or eleven years old, hopped briskly out and started for the playground, already crowding with children.

She glanced over her shoulder, a slim, pretty, breakable child, long, black hair flowing from beneath her helmet. Following her glance, I saw her parents' car pulling back into traffic, but I

hesitated. The girl was already working on the helmet's chin strap, peeling the helmet from her head and running her fingers through her hair to remove its crushing outline. She hid the helmet in her backpack and swung through the gateway bars of

Helmets

the playground, where she disappeared in a group of laughing girls.

The blare of the bus horn startled me so greatly I jerked forward without checking traffic, causing another, smaller, horn blast. A mother glared, the seats of her car filled with wide-eyed children. At the first available corner, I signalled and turned away, fleeing, having lost the white sedan during my study of their daughter—their daughter who didn't share their hopeless ideas of safety a second longer than necessary for appearances.

After driving pointlessly for several minutes, I headed back for the school. I wanted again to see that young girl, so like all the others, so childish looking, but already able to see with a clarity greater than her parents'.

But at the school the playground was empty, the children all safely inside, even the crossing guards heading for their cars, not to return until the lunchtime recess.

I didn't go to work that day, though I would have been little more than an hour late. For a long time I simply circled through town, hoping somehow that I might bump into the white sedan.

I considered going home, spending the day with Nancy, but I pictured sitting on the edge of the bed while she dressed for her afternoon at the school, clipping her earrings on, only half listening to the excuse I'd invented to explain being home in the middle of the day. Once she was gone, I'd walk through our house, my footsteps ringing off the hardwood floors, wondering for the first time how she filled all the hours.

It was nearly dark before I stopped my car in our driveway and spent the dinner hour telling Nancy what I'd accomplished at work that day.

The following morning, I again walked around the corner as if going to work. After waiting an appropriate time I returned home for the car keys, grumbling about missing the bus.

Pete Fromm

But this morning Nancy followed me out to the driveway. "Wilton?" she said, leaving it there for me to explain.

"What?" I asked, irritated by being forced to play simple.

"I don't remember you ever missing the bus before." She looked at me carefully, truly concerned. "Is everything all right? Everything at work?"

Ever since Mr. Becker had gone past the suggestion stage, I'd tried to come up with some way to tell Nancy about what they were still calling *early* retirement, though *forced* seemed considerably more accurate. But, after so long a time believing in my work, I didn't know what to say. I smiled at Nancy and shook my head. "Old-timer's disease," I said.

She smiled obediently, but it did little to dispel her worried expression. "You'd tell me, wouldn't you, Wilton? If there was something?"

I said, "Of course I would, Nancy."

She watched me back down the drive and, even after I turned the corner, I could feel her watching.

Worrying that people as careful as the Helmet family would surely recognize the same car following them in from the desert, I decided to wait for them at the daughter's school. My timing was off, perhaps due to my excitement, or my rush to get away from Nancy's questions, and I spent nearly half an hour parked in front of the school before the white sedan appeared.

I watched the girl repeat her movements of yesterday, as far as the unstrapping of the helmet, before I had to leave in order to follow the rest of her family. As I chased them across town, I wondered if the parents were at all aware of their daughter's duplicity. Or perhaps she was allowed to remove her helmet in school. Perhaps her parents were so adept at self-deception that they could imagine school as a safe haven, despite the contents of the nightly newscasts.

The car stopped at another school and even as I pulled in,

Helmets

several slots behind them, I wondered why the children attended different schools, schools so far apart. I had not yet had time to take in my surroundings.

Rather than the son simply leaping from the car as their daughter had, both front doors swung open. I nearly smiled at the recklessness of the move, the helmeted father actually stepping into the traffic lane. They met at the son's door and opened it for him. Then, together, they helped him toward the school door, his steps herky-jerky, decisionless, his head rolling this way and that, sometimes lolling as if its weight were simply too much for the thin neck.

Realizing what I was seeing, I averted my gaze, wiping at my forehead's sudden sheen of sweat, feeling little more than a Peeping Tom. Instead, I looked into the playground, awash with adults, more of them, it seemed, than children. Nearly all the children wore helmets, some much more severe than the son's white model, some heavy and leatherish, some even with faceguards, though the children never seemed out of catching range of an attendant, should their labored steps disintegrate into complete collapse.

At the door, as the parents stooped to kiss and pet him, I saw the unmistakable cast of the son's face, the features of whatever it is that causes all that.

The family disappeared inside for just a moment, then the parents reappeared alone, trotting to their car, hands fiddling with their chin straps. At the car, they flipped their helmets into the still-open door of the back seat. The father grazed a finger along his wife's shoulders as he moved around her on his way to the driver's seat and, though I'd planned to follow them, to see where they went next, I knew it was no longer necessary. I stayed where I was for quite some time, trying not to look into that awful playground, the white flash of the son's helmet unmistakable in the mass of globed heads.

I sat with my head down and my eyes closed until I'd regained some composure—an old trick of Nancy's—and then I eased into the street, wondering where to go. The quick tire screech was all the warning I had before the jolt and the sound of the metal.

The woman was flustered, but kind, more concerned with her helmeted daughter than any minor damage to her station wagon. I tried to give cash, but she laughed, saying a swap of insurance papers would be plenty. She seemed surprised not to know me, and was immediately standoffish when I said I wasn't here with a child. I followed her glance to the playground, where the attendants were trying to keep their flock from stumbling toward the excitement of our accident. I wondered for a horrified moment if there were people who actually came to gawk at these children and, without planning to, I said, "I'm new here. I'm still just checking into schools for our child."

I accompanied her all the way up the steps with her girl as she assured me that I could do no better than this school. The parents, too, were wonderful. And the support groups, if we were interested in that sort of thing. I said that indeed we were, my wife and I, and we formally introduced ourselves before returning to our cars, where I apologized once more.

I made it several blocks before pulling over and again lowering my head and closing my eyes.

I don't know how she managed it, if she'd been waiting by the window since I left or not, but Nancy was on the front step before I'd finished pulling into the driveway. Coming home in the middle of the morning, with the fender buckled, I knew there would have to be some explanation, but I'd been unable to collect my thoughts even toward a starting point.

Nancy met me at the car door, nearly blocking me in.

"Good morning," I said, sliding out and stepping around her toward the house. She was already dressed for her volunteer work with those children who'd never met a nice man.

Helmets

"Wilton?" she said, following. "What is it, Wilton?"

I was sweating and my hand trembled as I reached for the doorknob.

"What happened to the car, Wilton? Have you been hurt?"

At the edge of the dining-room table, I glanced around our modest house and then turned and looked at Nancy, my wife of thirty-seven years. "They're forcing me to retire," I said, out with it all at once.

Nancy stared. "But the car? Are you all right?"

I waved that away. "Retired," I repeated. "I'm going to lose my work."

"I know how much your work means to you, Wilton," she said quietly. "But that doesn't explain this. What's happened?"

"I've been following the Helmet family," I said, surprising myself. "The helmets. They're not for what we thought. That family knows more about safety than we ever will." Suddenly I needed to sit down. "My work, Nancy. It's all I've ever had."

"What about the Helmet family?" she asked, pulling up one of the dining-room chairs and sitting beside me.

Briefly, I told her what I'd seen, how they wore the helmets only so their boy wouldn't be alone. I even told about the woman who'd hit our car. "I had to lie to her," I said. "She thought I was just there to stare at those children."

"What did you tell her?" she whispered.

"I told her we had our own child. That I was simply looking for a place where he'd be welcome."

As I spoke, Nancy broke down and I held her and rocked her in those hard dining-room chairs, my head down over hers, my eyes closed tight.

Excerpts from

Buffalo, New York
July, 1875

SLEEP.

For all animated beings sleep is an imperious necessity, as indispensable as food. The welfare of man requires alternate periods of activity and repose. It is a well-established fact, that during the wakeful hours the vital energies are being expended, the powers of life diminished, and, if wakefulness is continued beyond a certain limit, the system becomes enfeebled and death is the result. During sleep there is a temporary cessation of vital expenditures, and a recuperation of all the forces. Under the influence of sleep the blood is refreshed, the brain recruited, physical sufferings are extinguished, mental troubles are removed, the organism is relieved, and hope returns to the heart.

Sleeping Rooms should be large and well ventilated, and the air kept moderately cool. The necessity for a fire may be determined by the health of the occupant. Besides maintaining a proper temperature in the room, a little fire is useful, especially if in a grate, for the purpose of securing good ventilation. The windows should not be so arranged as to allow a draught upon the body during the night, but yet so adjusted that the inmate may obtain plenty of fresh air.

The Bed should not be too soft, but rather hard. Feathers give off animal emanations of an injurious character, and impart a feeling of lassitude and debility to those sleeping on them. No more coverings should be used than are actually necessary for the comfort of the individual. Cotton sheets are warmer than linen, and answer equally as well.

Sleeping Alone. Certain effluvia are thrown off from our persons, and when two individuals sleep together each inhales from the other more or less of these emanations. There is little doubt that consumption, and many other diseases, not usually considered contagious, are sometimes communicated in this manner. When it is not practicable for individuals to occupy separate beds, the persons sleeping together should be of about the same age, and in good health. Numerous cases have occurred in which healthy, robust children have gradually declined and died within a few months, from the evil effects of sleeping with old people. Again, those in feeble health have been greatly benefited, and even restored, by sleeping with others who were young and healthy.

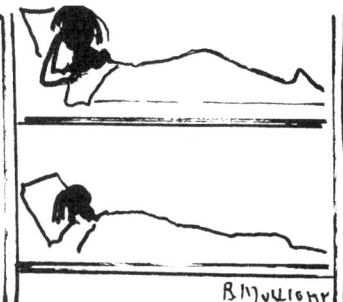

Time for Sleep. Night is the proper time for sleep. When day is substituted for night, the sleep obtained does not fully restore the exhausted energies of the system. Nature does not allow her laws to be broken with impunity.

Position in Sleep. The proper position in sleep is upon the right side. The orifice leading from the stomach to the bowels being on this side, this position favors the passage of the contents into the duodenum. Lying on the back is injurious, since by so doing the spine becomes heated, especially if the person sleeps on feathers, the circulation is obstructed and local congestions are encouraged. The face should never be covered during sleep, since it necessitates the breathing of the same air over again, together with the emanations from the body.

Editors' note: So now you know.

Tony Eprile

This picture was taken at Scottsburgh Beach on the Natal coast. I'm the blond clutching either a toy or some primitive weapon. My family used to go to the same hotel, the Lido in Umkomaas, every year, since it was one of the few South African hotels that would allow children to eat with their parents. The beach had wonderful tidepools—probably what I'm musing on in the photo—and, for some reason, I remember the advertisement for Cutty Sark "Scots whiskey" as you drove up to the parking area. The name Cutty Sark still calls up for me the strong scent of Natal beaches, a heady combination of salt, burnt sugarcane fields, and sun-baked seaweed.

Tony Eprile grew up in South Africa, where his father was founding editor of the country's first mass-circulation multiracial newspaper, the *Golden City Post*. He is the author of *Temporary Sojourner & Other South African Stories*.

Eprile has lived on the East and West coasts and now sojourns temporarily in the Midwest, where he teaches writing and African literature at Northwestern University.

TONY EPRILE
The Entrepreneurs

They pulled off the highway in a spurt of dust and gravel. "That's the road up there." The driver of the Zola pointed to the opposite side of the motorway. "You just walk, walk, walk until you get to where the peach tree used to be, then you follow your left hand past some koppies and tin huts. You'll find your man there, I promise you."

The Toyota minivan darted back onto the highway again, causing a speeding Mercedes to swerve sharply and hoot in anger. The van beep-beeped cheerily in reply, or perhaps simply as encouragement to Naboth, who watched it recede into the distance. On the van's back panel was a slogan lovingly hand-painted in gold lettering: "RODE TO RICHES."

"You can talk," Naboth spoke out loud, thinking bitterly of the three five-rand notes he had handed the jovial driver. These minivan taxis—which were known by the ironic name of Zola Budds because they moved fast, stopped suddenly, and had a habit of knocking people over—provided a good livelihood. The trouble was, you didn't try to break in uninvited...not if you had the ordinary kind of human skin that could be penetrated by sharp objects.

Gauging an interval in the stream of fast-moving traffic, Naboth ran across the highway, his Natal Leather Company

Tony Eprile

suitcase banging against the side of his leg. He started up the gravel road cheerily enough, pausing only to remove the sharp-edged stones that kept slipping into his city shoes. He would have liked to take the shoes off to save their finish, but years in town had sloughed away the habit of walking barefoot. After about a mile of painful hiking, he passed a group of women going the other way. They waved and smiled at him and he envied the ease with which they balanced their burdens on their heads and benefited from the resulting shade. A hundred yards or so farther on, there was the ping of flying brass studs as the suitcase handle came unmoored. The heavy bag wrenched out of his grasp, spraining the muscle of his upper arm. Naboth rubbed the injured spot ruefully, looked back to make sure none of the women was watching, and then seized the suitcase in both hands and headed into the veld. He slipped it under a thicket of thornbush, adding several more branches to better conceal it. As he stepped back, there was a tearing sound: the sleeve of his polyester jacket had snagged on a thorn. A light line of displaced threads ran through the darker blue.

He walked on, cursing the heat, the dust that parched his throat, the plants that pricked and cut and jabbed his tender flesh. A world without shelter or shade, that was rural life! He heard a car grinding its way up the road in the direction he was taking, and he stuck his thumb out hopefully, only to be given an angry glare by the pale-fleshed woman who was driving. He cursed her and the car, too, but carefully, when it was not likely that anyone glancing into the rearview mirror could see him doing so. This was the countryside, after all, where things are different in that they haven't changed.

Naboth paused at the top of a hill, his eyes stinging as sweat dripped into them, the land around shimmering in the heat. You could die here easily, of sunstroke or thirst, and all that would be left would be a dried-out shell like the broken white cases of dead millipedes. No one would know; only the State, after a few

The Entrepreneurs

years, would note the inactivity of your bank account and swallow up the contents. Naboth wandered down a barely discernible footpath to relieve himself, amazed that his body still contained any superfluous liquid. As he zipped up, he realized that the stump overgrown with sawgrass must be the former peach tree the driver had told him about. That idiot! How was anyone who'd never been there in the first place supposed to know to turn off where something isn't there anymore? How was this country ever going to prosper if people couldn't even give you decent directions? Perhaps it was a good omen, though. The ancestors had tickled his bladder at just the right moment and saved him from wandering uselessly down this hellish road.

He continued on slowly, squinting his eyes to avoid the glare. Yes, there were the koppies, standing tall like welcoming sentinels to either side of him. The road meandered past a brownish, evil-looking stream, its narrow trickle of water foaming unnaturally with runoff fertilizer from the surrounding farmland. At last, there were some tin-roofed huts and, lying on his side in the sparse shade of a thinly leaved tree, was a man wearing what clearly were once city clothes: a dusty pair of charcoal-gray trousers, a faded blue Oxford shirt.

"Hey, my friend," Naboth called, his voice unnaturally loud in the stillness of the afternoon. "Can you provide me with something to drink? I think my head is going to burst and fly off in a thousand pieces."

The man listlessly pointed toward a jerry can resting against the side of the hut. Naboth took the tin mug from the top of the jerry can, poured some acrid-smelling water into it, and drank gratefully. He refilled the cup and poured some of the liquid over his left wrist to cool himself, only to be interrupted by an angry shout from the man under the tree. "Hey, stranger. Drink, but don't waste! You think you just turn on a tap around here?"

"Excuse me, I wasn't thinking."—And you needn't have talked so sharply, either. You live in the country, but you know nothing of the laws of hospitality—"Are you by any chance Teacher Makize?"

The man laughed bitterly. "You can call me that, but I haven't been in a school for a year now. And I won't be in front of a classroom again if the DET has anything to say about it." A suspicious look appeared on his face. "How do you know who I am? What do you want from me?"

"It's all right, baba. I was sent by your cousin Sipho."

The man sank wearily back into his former posture. "What's that troublemaker done now?"

"He told me you could help me get rich like him. I want a secret like the spell you gave Sipho."

"Sipho? He's not rich. Not unless he's been stealing." The man's voice rose a pitch in irritation.

"Hai, baba! I've seen his Mercedes. It was bright and clean and shone like a mirror. He was on his way to pick up his girlfriend to take her to a *restaurant* and to a drive-in cinema!"

"Oh, god. Sipho's lying to you. Even when he was this small, he was a big, big liar."

"No, you have it wrong. I saw the car with my own eyes. Sipho said he got the secret to get rich from you. I want you to help me, so I can get money, too." Naboth took another cup of water and squatted down on his heels to show his patience. He knew the man wouldn't turn over his secret just for the asking, but he wasn't leaving until he got the answer he wanted.

"So Sipho told you I gave him some medicine, some *muti*, and that's how he acquired all his wealth?"

"That's right. Now I'm here." If you persist, they always come around. Just persist, persist. "I'll give you my wristwatch—Timex—for this medicine. It cost me a hundred rand."

The teacher's eyes flickered, his guess that Naboth was a Zulu confirmed by his pronunciation of the English words: *a hundled iLandi*. The headmaster of Makize's school had been a Zulu, and stubborn just like this one. "What am I going to do with a

The Entrepreneurs

wristwatch out here? Tell how much time I have to hang out doing nothing in the middle of nowhere?" The former teacher spat into the red dust at his side. "Keep your bloody watch, man. I'll tell you the secret. But then you must promise to leave right away and never bother me again."

"Thank you, my friend. I am too happy!"

"Okay, but it's not easy. You have to work to get rich, you know that? You have to accomplish a task, or the *muti* won't work. Come over here!" The teacher spoke with a new firm tone of command. Pleased, Naboth went and sat down before him. The other man dipped a finger into the tin cup, rubbed the wet finger into the red dust, and drew two parallel lines on Naboth's forehead. "First of all, you have to lose your name…"

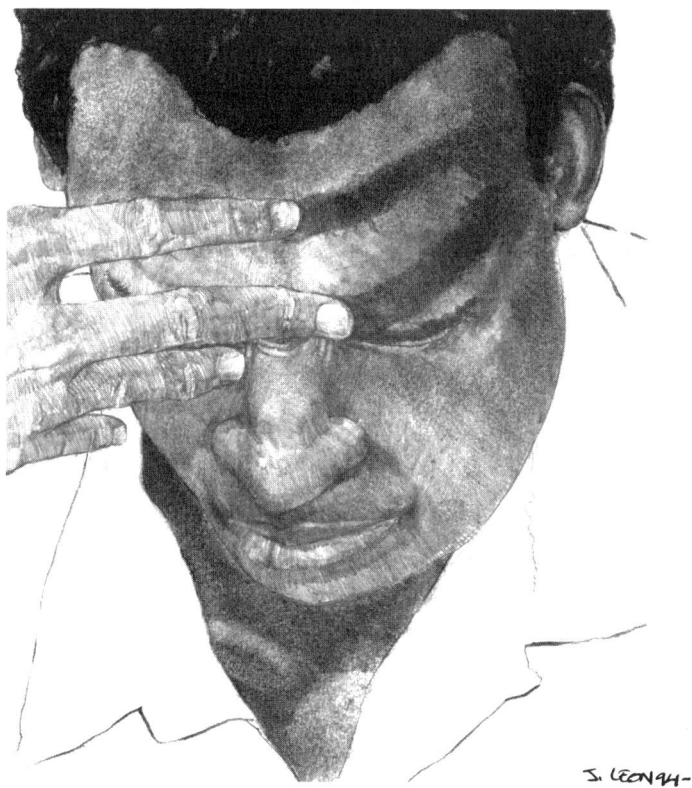

Tony Eprile

"My name?"

"Yes. From now until four Sundays from now, you cannot have a name. Throw away your identity card. And if anyone asks your name, you can't just make up a new one, you have to tell them you don't have any name."

"That's hard…" Naboth murmured. He didn't like the idea of getting rid of his identity card.

"Well, you don't have to do any of this," the teacher said impatiently. "You can go home, go about your business, forget this nonsense about getting rich."

"No, no, I will do it. Is that everything?"

"There's one more thing; after the fourth Sunday, you must go home to KwaZulu and stay there. Any business you put your hand to will prosper after that. Provided you fulfill the conditions exactly as I told you. Now, go!"

Naboth carefully placed his wristwatch on the other man's lap—you always paid for medicine, otherwise it wouldn't work—then he stood, nodded respectfully, and began walking back down the path with jaunty steps.

"Why did you tell him those lies, you useless?" a woman said, coming out of the hut.

"It's Sipho's fault. You know how he always plays practical jokes. I'll bet you he told this idiot that his employer's Mercedes was his own. How else was I supposed to get rid of him? Besides, the crazy stranger drank up all the water." The man strapped Naboth's watch around his own wrist. It was a perfect fit.

"Nevertheless, you shouldn't have told him to throw away his identity card," the woman grumbled.

The teacher waved her words away as if he were shooing flies, then lay back in the shade to rest.

The man walked down the gravel road, each step taking him farther from his identity card. He had overturned a large rock about a hundred yards back, brushed away the earwigs and

The Entrepreneurs

woodlice that were lurking underneath, and dug a small hole. As soon as he took the ID card out of his wallet, it began objecting. "What do you think you're doing?" it said. "If you lose me, you'll be in deep trouble!" Amazingly, it spoke in exactly the clipped English tones of the sergeant of police who had stopped the man's father on the way back from a church service many years before. As he wrapped the little plastic square in a paper handkerchief, he remembered watching his father's growing terror as he searched first the right inside pocket of his jacket, then the left, while the policeman berated him in this same voice. Carefully, he placed the rock over the small declivity that now contained his identity.

"Come back at once or you'll be sorry," he heard the voice in his ears, fainter now. It was not too late to turn back. He had made some scratches on the stone with his nail trimmers, and he would still be able to identify it among all the other rocks. Half a mile farther on, he knew that that was it; he was not going back. He felt a peculiar lifting of his spirits, a sense of freedom that he had never felt before. All his adult life he had carried some form of official document, first the hated passbook, the *dompas*, with its rubber stamps and employer endorsement, then the identity card, less hateful but still coded for race and ethnic origin. Now he had nothing. He strode easily, his shoulders squared back, his step firm. The sun was not quite so high now, and the heat was less bothersome than before. Even his suitcase, when he retrieved it, felt lighter than it had earlier, and he was able to rig up an improvised carrying strap with the canvas belt to his other pair of trousers. He felt ready to start a new life.

He turned left when he reached the motorway, heading out toward Natal but with no clear destination in mind. After he had been walking for a while, he paused for a moment to rest. It was just as well that he did, because a string of fast-moving bicyclists came pouring out from behind a hedge that hid another side road. With their white helmets, plastic goggles, Lycra bodysuits,

Tony Eprile

their awkward postures hunched over the expensive racing bikes, and the strident whirring of their tires, they resembled some sort of large, swift insects... locusts, perhaps. Watching them pass, Naboth admired the precision of their limbs, the rapidity of their progress. He hoisted up his suitcase and stepped forth again on his own way, but as he passed the side road, he was halted by a shout and a rush of wind past his face. The straggler, who had narrowly missed running into him, skidded where the road surface changed from Tarmac to gravel. The rider almost regained his balance, but the angle was too steep and, as if in slow motion, he fell to one side while the bicycle shot into the roadway under the wheels of a passing goods lorry.

Naboth stared at the unconscious cyclist who lay prostrate almost at his very feet. Behind him, he could hear the belated screech of brakes and the cries and yells of African workers who had been waiting for a bus on the other side of the road. He felt as if he saw the injured man from very far off—an absurd figure lying in the dirt like a shotgunned guinea fowl. There were more shouts, the sound of running feet, further shrieking brakepads as cars slowed to avoid hitting the erstwhile bus passengers who ran without heed across the busy road. Naboth caught the eye of the terrified lorry driver, who had now reversed and had stuck his head out of the window to see what he'd hit. "Aiii, you killed him!" a man shouted, reaching the prone body. "You hit him and you killed him." Naboth could see decision take shape on the driver's face; there was a grinding of gears and the lorry hurtled out onto the motorway and sped away.

Naboth leaned down and unbuckled the strap to the cyclist's helmet. He gently extricated the man's head and removed the helmet with its yellow foam padding, soft and secure as the inside of a weaverbird's nest. The cyclist's eyelids fluttered and he gave a faint sigh. The crowd pressing around Naboth murmured in satisfaction at these signs of life. "Shame," a woman's voice said, "that bloody driver didn't even stop."

The Entrepreneurs

The cyclist sat up and looked around in surprise at the crowd of African faces peering down at him. "What's going on?" he asked conversationally, causing a subdued titter.

"What's going on is that you are coming off your bicycle," Naboth replied, causing a few members of the crowd to laugh outright. He hadn't meant to make a joke, but already the crowd behind him were repeating the exchange for the benefit of newcomers. At this moment, a police car passing on the other side of the road performed a U-turn across two lanes and skidded to a halt near them. A young white officer and an African constable got out and approached the crowd. A minivan with the words "Raleigh Racing Tour" made the same U-turn and pulled up behind the police car.

"What's the disturbance?" the white policeman demanded, unconsciously tugging at his Sam Browne belt.

"This man was run over by a lorry and now he has come back to life," a man in the crowd responded. "It is a miracle of God."

"I fell off my effing bike," the cyclist said, standing up painfully. "And this idiot thinks it's funny!" He pointed at Naboth, who looked around for some support against this injustice. No one else seemed ready to come to his aid—the crowd was watching him with interest in anticipation of new signs of wit; the policemen were staring at him with officious distrust; the only people not looking at him were two men in white overalls who had gotten out of the minivan and who were carefully straightening out the bent front rim of the bicycle.

"I saw you fall down... I was worried about you," he tried to explain. The two men in white overalls came up to the cyclist and began feeling his legs and arms with the same assiduous care they had shown toward the bicycle.

By now, the policeman had taken out a notebook and a stubby pencil. "You were a witness to the accident?"

"Yes. I was standing here. He came down the hill very fast..."

"He was run over by a big truck," interrupted the same man

who had spoken up earlier. "It is God's will that he's not dead."

"First he fell off, then a lorry ran over the bike," Naboth hurriedly interjected.

"And then you started making jokes," the cyclist said, advancing angrily toward Naboth. "I hit my head; I wreck a four-thousand-rand bike, and you think it's a big bloody joke. Ha! Ha!"

One of the overalled men, who had an Australian accent and a distinct black handprint in chain grease on his bleached pants, succeeded in calming the errant rider and convincing him that they could replace the tire "quicker than a wombat's fart" and get him back on the tour. The policeman, meanwhile, was getting increasingly frustrated at the divergent descriptions of the hit-and-run vehicle: a gray minivan, a lorry fetching lumber from the Houtkop mill up the road, a dusty white Ford pickup. "You can't leave," he told the cyclist. "I has to file a report."

"Sorry, mate," the Australian said. "No time for that. Just forget about it."

"I has to make a report," the officer complained, but the other white men insistently ignored him as they climbed into the Raleigh minivan. In frustration, the policeman ordered the crowd to disperse, telling them they were creating an illegal assembly.

"Not you," he said, grabbing Naboth's arm. "I needs your name for the report."

"I can't tell you my name, sir," Naboth replied.

"Stop your nonsense, my boy. You is my witness. Give me your name and address and then you can bugger off."

"I can't tell you that," Naboth said sorrowfully. The officer had gotten quite red in the face by now and was clearly on the verge of losing his temper.

"Right," he said, pushing Naboth toward the police car. "Obstructing justice, resisting arrest, and I'll think of something else, too. You're going to laugh on the other side of your face,

The Entrepreneurs

you skellum."

Naboth found himself in the back seat of the police car, behind the wire grille. The African policeman plunked himself beside him, folded his arms so that his hands accentuated the bulge of biceps beneath his short-sleeved shirt, and eyed Naboth ironically from just an inch or two away. "What have I done wrong?" Naboth asked plaintively, but the African policeman just continued to peer at him in this intimidating way and the driver, too, said nothing, his pimpled neck flaming red with exasperation.

When they finally arrived at the police station, the black policeman stuck a mallet-sized fist beneath Naboth's nose and murmured, "Now you're going to shit."

Naboth's hands were roughly forced behind his back and cuffed at the wrists, then he was left alone in a small anteroom. In the next room over, he could hear a senior officer telling off the policeman who had arrested him. "Three murders in the township last week, a patrol car shot at, and what do you do? You bring in a nameless witness to an accident that never happened!" The man's voice rose in a high insistent whine, tireless as a lone mosquito in a darkened room. After enjoying his excoriation of the young cop for some time, the senior officer came in and looked at Naboth.

"Okay, Nkabi," he said to the African constable, "take him to the fingerprint room and get his prints. We'll put them in the computer and find out soon enough if our friend here is a terrorist. And, Nkabi, maybe if you ask him nicely he'll tell you his name."

Steely fingers gripped his sprained arm by the elbow and Naboth fell over his own feet as he was thrust down the stairs leading to the fingerprint room. The handcuffs were removed and his hands crammed first against an ink pad, then against a white sheet of paper—the four fingers crunched down and rotated separately from the thumb—to leave a clear and unsmudged impress, tribute to the policeman's practiced art. He was handed a rag smelling evilly of turpentine, and then the black constable stood before him, very close, a newly sharpened pencil still smelling of wood shavings in one hand, a clipboard in the other.

"Your name?"

"I'm sorry—" Naboth's words were lost in the sudden expulsion of his breath as the blunt end of the pencil was rammed, stiletto-like, into his solar plexus. He doubled over, his face meeting a rapidly rising knee in a meld of brilliant light, deep blackness, and scalding flesh.

"You think you're hard, but you're soft, soft, soft. I can break you like that!" Nkabi said, snapping the pencil neatly in two. Naboth lay quietly, his face pulsing with waves of heat, salt liquid burning its way down his throat. When he was able to focus again, the first objects that came into sight were the constable's muscular calves and shiny, reinforced leather boots. He was going to have to do something before those boots trampled over him.

"Listen, there's a reason I can't tell you my name. It has to do with a Sangoma."

"Don't talk lies. When you open your mouth, worms fall out."

"Seriously. This is the truth, not worms." The booted feet shuffled impatiently, and Naboth sped up the course of his tale despite the pain from his swelling lips. "I hired a Sangoma to help me dream a lucky number for the Fah-Fee, but I only paid her half. 'As sure as my name is my name,' I said, 'I'll give you the remainder when I get my Friday paypacket.'

"Well, I didn't win. And I thought to myself: this one's medicine is not good, why should I pay her the rest of the money? A few days later I went out to buy some beer, but it was very hot and I got confused. I wandered all over the township without finding the shop, and then, when I opened a door that

The Entrepreneurs

I thought was it, there was the Sangoma waiting for me. 'You swear too lightly on your name,' she told me. 'The next time you open your mouth to say your name, you will die. And the person who asked you your name, they will die, too.'"

"This is more rubbish. Am I wearing a blanket that you think I'm some stupid country bumpkin?" The voice drifting down to Naboth was angry, but the feet did not kick him.

A few moments later, the young white cop came in. He stopped abruptly when he saw the broken pencil. "Ag, Nkabi, what did you do that for? You think pencils is grown on trees?"

"It can still be used," the other replied morosely.

"Nooo, man. And what am I supposed to tell Captain Van Rooyen when he wants to know why we use up more supplies than anyone else? And what about this joker; did you find out his name?"

"He has forgotten his name. Truly." The black constable tapped his head with his finger significantly.

"'Strue? I saw a film like that. This guy goes outside one day and somebody hits him on the head and he gets ammonia. He doesn't know who he is anymore. Then this nice rich lady takes care of him and they fall in love. Just when they're going to get married, a flowerpot falls out of a window and hits him on the head, and he remembers everything—his name, his bloody nagging wife, and screaming, bratty children—and he has to tell the nice lady he can't marry her even though he loves her. Ag, I cried when that happened. I couldn't help it. You know, maybe if we hit this guy on the head again, he'll remember who he is." He peered down at Naboth and asked in an unnaturally loud voice: "Who are you? What is your name?"

"Please, boss, I don't know."

The following morning, Naboth was arraigned on charges of vagrancy, resisting arrest, and loitering with the intent of creating a public nuisance. The examining magistrate, the

TONY EPRILE

Honorable Brits Van Stossel, pondered the prisoner in the dock while he calculated how much work was still needed on his terraced garden. Despite his city clothes, this miscreant had broad shoulders and strong hands and, like most Africans, was probably quite used to physical labor.

"Four weeks. To be spent on work detail, not idling around at government expense!" The magistrate was not through yet, though, for presently he addressed the young white policeman. "Perhaps, Officer Botha, if it's not too much trouble, you might consider devoting a little of your precious time to chasing a real criminal now and then?"

This remark made Constable Nkabi chuckle under his breath, and his hold on Naboth's upper arm while leading him out of the courtroom was not quite so fierce. "You're lucky," Nkabi said to him. "Now you'll get to answer to a number and you won't have to worry about your name until we let you out again."

The Honorable Brits Van Stossel's substantial white brick house sat atop a small rise. The native flora of scrubby underbrush had been plucked and shaved into near invisibility, replaced with carefully tended green lawns and baked flower beds, smelling richly of black, peat-enriched humus. The shape of the hill itself had been changed by tasteful brick terracing that kept the cherished flower beds from washing away in the area's violent downpours. Naboth found his place in a crew of three (supervised by a bored warder armed with a high-powered rifle), who were reinforcing the lowest tier of the garden at the edge of the property. Naboth's job was to pass bricks from a wheelbarrow to Stokvels, a wiry South Sotho with a peppering of silver in his hair and a fixed, anxious smile. Stokvels then handed the brick to Spaza, a brawny younger man from the local township, who carefully set it in place before using a trowel to scrape off any excess cement. Naboth could see that Spaza was using too much mortar—it would contract as it dried and begin

The Entrepreneurs

to crack from the contrasting heat and chill of passing days and nights—but he did not bother to say anything. The other two were already annoyed with him because he refused to tell them his name, and he did not want to reiterate the Sangoma story: these things have a habit of coming true with the saying of them. He did not mind that they relegated him to the worst job: wheeling the heavy barrow back and forth from the prison pickup when fresh bricks were needed. It took the edge off their suspiciousness of him.

"Hell, I could use a Castle lager right now," Stokvels said, wiping sweat from his forehead with the side of his arm. He had made this remark about once every half hour. "A nice barrowful of ice-cold cans instead of this load of focking bricks."

Spaza took the brick handed to him and mimed flipping the top of it open, then pretended to pour cool liquid down his throat. "To your health," he declared, holding up the rough, red brick. He had a deep, gravelly voice, like that of "the lion," Mahlathini.

"Don't even joke like that," Stokvels grumbled. "A couple weeks ago, I could walk over to my refrigerator any time I wanted and pull out a nice cold one. That's what got that bastard local policeman, Thomas Kakala, to jealous me. He told me that he had also bought a fridge on the hire purchase. He told me exactly how much he had to pay each month. 'That's nice,' I said to him. 'Enjoy it.' I knew he wanted me to give him money, but the hell! I let him come free to my house; I let him drink all the beer he wanted."

"Where did you get so rich?" Naboth asked.

"NoName speaks! When NoName speaks, Nobody listens." Stokvels laughed a surprisingly shrill laugh. "I wasn't rich yet, but I was on the path; my feet were on the path. It's easy what I did: I bought a television from a friend in town. I put up chairs, served cold beer, brewed my own liquor. M-Net! Sports! Orlando Pirates versus the Umtata Bucks! Then that Kakala turned me in. No license for the television, no license for the liquor, no license for the chairs, no license for being without a license. I'm drinking bricks now, and I'm going to be drinking bricks for a long time."

"It's your own fault," Spaza asserted. "Kakala has to eat. You've got to bribe. It's as simple as that. I'm a businessman. I *know*."

"You're a businessman? Busy with a trowel," Stokvels sneered. Spaza looked as if he were ready to take the little man's head and slap it on the mortar in place of the next brick.

"Hey, we're all here, all in the same shit," Naboth interjected, seeking to make peace. "Tell me how you were a businessman."

"Everybody has to eat, that's my motto. I was selling food boxes to the people who had to commute to work. Early, early, I was out there when the Zolas were waiting with their engines running. People knew, those commuters knew they could get breakfast from me and eat it on the drive. They could sleep a few minutes longer and not have to be hungry all day. When they came back from work, they could buy dinner and not have to go home and start the charcoal or fire up the gas. I had seven women working for me. I had boerewors. I had chicken. I had putu, Ting, you name it. Everybody's got to eat."

"Then some Kakala turned you in, right?" Stokvels said glumly.

"Nobody turned me in. I gave the drivers free, the best food. I gave the police free. Everybody's got to eat. You bribe, you stay in business. No, man, it's because I have a temper. This one guy, he didn't want to pay up. A couple of weeks I let him go; he said he hadn't been paid. No problem. Lots of people, they didn't have money this week, they gave me the end of next week. You don't want to be too tight. Then I told him: 'My friend, it's time.' 'The food was bad,' he said. He had to throw the chicken out the window. Why should he pay for chicken with maggots in it? He said all this with my other customers standing where they

The Entrepreneurs

could hear. I cut him, man. I cut him fast. He didn't even see it coming, just blood, and then him squealing like a pig."

"Au, that's hard," Stokvels said, regret at his earlier rash remark explicit on his face.

"No, I'm fair. If someone's hungry, pay me tomorrow. Everybody's got to eat. If it wasn't for that thief, I'd still be in business."

"When I get free from here, I'm going to start up again. I'll get a license for everything, and Kakala can go to hell," Stokvels mused. "Maybe I'll even serve food."

"Food is the best. Soon as I'm free, I'm back to business. Everybody's got to eat. But I got thirty months for cutting that guy. It's hard."

"I got one year, and I lost all my money. But I'll start again. You can't lose with television, 'specially sports." He looked over at Naboth, who pretended disinterest but had been drinking in every word. "What about you, NoName? What are you going to do when they let you go?"

Naboth smiled mysteriously. "I have my plans," he said softly.

"Sure," his companions jeered in unison. "NoName has plans!"

Siobhan Dowd, program director of PEN American Center's Freedom-to-Write Committee, writes this column regularly, alerting readers to the plight of writers around the world who deserve our awareness and our writing action.

Writer Detained: Ken Saro-Wiwa
by Siobhan Dowd

Ken Saro-Wiwa, a member of the Ogoni people of southern Nigeria and the president of MOSOP (Movement for the Survival of the Ogoni People), recently wrote the following SOS from his prison cell:

> This is an attempt to destroy me, MOSOP, and all the Ogoni people. The entire leadership of MOSOP is either in detention, on the wanted list, or dead. Ogoni villages have all been invaded by the marauding Nigerian army and burning, looting, rape, and murder are the order of the day.

These sad words reached the West in July 1994, two months after Saro-Wiwa's May 22 arrest—his fifth detention since 1993—upon his return from traveling abroad. During his absence, General Sani Abacha staged a successful coup, bringing to an abrupt end all promise of a successful and speedy transition to democracy.

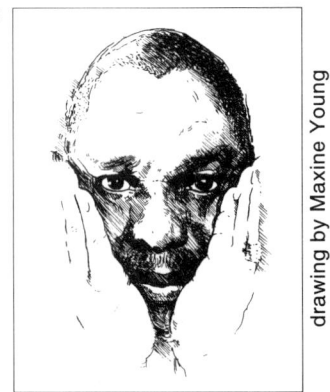

Ken Saro-Wiwa

drawing by Maxine Young

Writer Detained: Ken Saro-Wiwa

Saro-Wiwa's untiring defense of the Ogoni people, a 150,000-strong minority living in the oil-rich, fabulously beautiful Niger Delta in Nigeria's south, is without doubt the sole reason that he has been so continually harassed by successive Nigerian governments. As a leader of MOSOP, he claims that the oil multinationals, such as Shell and Chevron, along with Nigeria's military government, are responsible for the environmental degradation of the Ogoni homeland over the years, and he has pointed out that his people have been denied their rightful royalties from the oil revenues. Today, if Saro-Wiwa's prison sources are to be believed, the Ogoni people face extermination at the hands of General Abacha's marauding army.

Aged 52, Saro-Wiwa was born in Rivers State in the south, to one of the three wives of James Wiwa. He attended the government college in Umuahia and then the University of Ibadan, where he graduated in English. During the Biafran War, he walked across the war zone to escape, and later received various government appointments, culminating in a spell as commissioner for information and home affairs.

As well as being an environmental campaigner, Saro-Wiwa is one of Nigeria's most popular writers and a founder of Nigerian PEN. He is the author of the country's most popular soap opera, *Basi & Company*, about a fatally flawed hero who is constantly dreaming up new schemes to get rich quick. His extraordinary novel *Sozaboy*, written in a carefully crafted mix of idiomatic English and pidgin English, was hailed by the British author William Boyd in a 1993 article in the *London Times* as "one of the great achievements of African literature." The book, praised for its daring use of language, follows the misfortunes of a raw recruit in a civil war, who sees his village and family devastated.

Asked recently by a representative of PEN, the writers' group, if he ever has trouble getting into print, Saro-Wiwa explained that he prints all his books himself, since they are published by the Saros International Limited company, which he founded

Siobhan Dowd

and directs. He has also written an anthology of poems, a collection of short stories, and several radio plays and children's books, and has won a number of prizes for his work.

In 1990, Saro-Wiwa turned his attention to political activism. President Babangida had made repeated promises for pluralistic elections, and the country, amid outbreaks of violent clashes between different ethnic groups, seemed at long last to be moving out of its pattern of military regimes and coups. Claiming that the Ogoni people should boycott the elections unless full provision in the constitution were made for the rights of minorities, Saro-Wiwa founded MOSOP and became president of the Ethnic Minority Rights Organization of Africa.

On April 2, 1993, he was detained by twenty police while on his way to give a lecture to students. A few days later, police came to his house, searching, they said, for an Ogoni flag. On April 15, he was detained once again. On June 21, he was formally arrested and charged with sedition and unlawful assembly, along with other MOSOP activists. His arrest came at a time when President Babangida had announced that the long-promised presidential elections were to be canceled.

During his last stay in prison in 1993, Saro-Wiwa kept a haunting prison diary. The following extract reflects his views very poignantly:

> Left alone amidst the stink of the cell, my mind wanders over recent events. Researching and writing my civil war diary, *On a Darkling Plain*, I had to come to the conclusion that if Nigeria is to continue to exist, there will have to be fundamental changes in the political structure of the country. Although my studies indicate that there is truly no reason for the existence of the country, I remain convinced that we must make an effort, in the interest of the black man, to make this accident of history work. But, we should return to the true nature of our society, the independence of the many ethnic nations, and form a federation—moving away from the unitary system which the military dictators are foisting on the country and which is driving everybody to perdition.

Writer Detained: Ken Saro-Wiwa

On that occasion, Saro-Wiwa was released after four weeks, three days after suffering a heart attack and after an international campaign on his behalf.

Although he has not yet been charged or tried, Saro-Wiwa predicts that the new government will keep him in prison for at least three years this time. *Glimmer Train* readers are encouraged to write letters to their local senators, representatives, and newspapers, and to Nigeria's current leader, pleading for Saro-Wiwa's release.

> General Sani Abacha
> Chairman, Provisional Ruling Council
> Commander-in-Chief of the Armed Forces and
>   Minister of Defense
> State House
> Abuja
> Federal Capital Territory
> NIGERIA

Janice Levy

The fact that I come down to earth from time to time enables me to jump even higher. My childhood dream was to play center field for the Yankees. I'm still waiting for the call.

Janice Levy has published over two dozen stories in literary magazines, such as the *American Voice*, *North Dakota Review*, *Vincent Brothers Review*, the *Sun*, and the *Alaska Quarterly*. Her work appears in the anthologies *If I Had My Life to Live Over*, *Lovers*, *The Time of Our Lives*, *Breaking Up Is Hard to Do*, and *Blessings and Bruises*. Two children's books, *The Adventures of Filimina Frog* and *Abuelito Goes Home*, were published in 1994.

Levy lives in Merrick, New York. She goes to baseball games with her husband, Rick, and children, Michael and Jahnna.

JANICE LEVY
Blue Paper Napkin

Three days after Maria Santana died, she spoke to her daughter at the bus stop.

"Lili," she hissed, her voice misty and low. "In the pink envelope. Behind the lotto stubs. Look again. Quick, before the *guagua* comes. You missed something."

Lili unzipped her shoulder bag and poked through her mother's things. She shook a ripped pink envelope, and a black-and-white photograph fell out, torn at one corner as if bitten. A skinny teenager in a *guayabera* shirt was almost as tall as the coconut tree he posed under.

"Is it—"

"No, it's not." The photograph moved slightly and Lili felt a warm breeze on her neck. "He left. Just moved away one day and that was that. He begged me to go with him, but I wouldn't. I couldn't. I was fifteen. I was scared."

"Did you ever—"

"Years later. In a McDonald's. He was even taller and so handsome that I couldn't breathe."

"Did you—"

"I couldn't. He ordered a Big Mac and a large chocolate shake. Then he brought them out to his car to a pregnant woman with a yellow hat. He took off her shoes and rubbed her feet. She wiped her lipstick off her straw, then slid it between his lips. He kissed her with a mouth full of hamburger. I hid behind a bush until they drove away."

Lili thought of her father returning to Puerto Rico, pale and thin each Christmas, homesick for the palm trees of *la isla* and the things her mother could do with plantains. Her mother wore pink nightgowns and fuzzy slippers and they cuddled on the couch in the middle of the afternoon. Her father rubbed her mother's back as she sat between his knees, laughter splashing down her face as they got drunk on rum and Cokes. Lili dropped dishes, lit matches, and made the bathtub overflow. When her father flew back to Brooklyn, Lili felt only a stillness inside her, a black space of relief.

"Did Papi—"

"No. There was no point."

"But you loved Papi."

"Of course."

"But still?"

"Still."

Lili felt a moist pressure on her cheek and inhaled the familiar spicy-sweet smell of *sofrito* and oranges. She climbed on the bus and took an *empanadilla* from her shoulder bag. Shivering, she ate the fried turnover in three bites.

"I missed you," Lili's husband says. He has flown back from another art show in Manhattan, this time with boxes of *santos* to sell here in the galleries of Ponce and Old San Juan.

"Look at this one." He caresses the wooden figure of a saint. "The Virgin of Montserrat. She stood in front of a bull in Homigueros and saved a farmer's life. I'd do that for you, you know." He flares his nostrils, puts his fingers to his head like horns, and kisses Lili hard on the lips.

"This one is for you," he says, unrolling a blue velvet cloth.

Blue Paper Napkin

"It's a *cachetones*. Look at her fat cheeks, her puffy face. Like when you stuff everything in your mouth so fast I'm afraid you'll blow up. She looks like you. My little fat cheeks."

He cups Lili's face in his hands and laughs, then suddenly stops. "What?" she says.

"The way I love you," he shrugs. "How easy it is. Like breathing."

Later Lili rubs his chest, taking little bites between his ribs.

"I hate being away from you. I hate anything that gets in the way of this," he sighs. "Can we sleep like this? All wrapped in each other? That's how much I love you. I know I can fall asleep first and you won't do me in."

Lili tickles the hairy base of her husband's spine while she imagines how Dickie Jon's back would feel against her breasts. She has seen the black hair on his chest and knows that it gets thicker on its way down to the top of his pants. She has watched him wipe his sweaty face, peel off his uniform shirt and throw it, with his eyes closed, over the top of the dugout. It is like a cockfight Lili thinks, as his blue and white number 27 is pecked apart by fans. She has never felt Dickie Jon's back, but she is sure it is bearlike and rippled.

Lili is startled by her husband's low moan. She wonders how long her hands have been massaging him below the waist. "You are so beautiful," he repeats.

Lili puts her fingers in his mouth and warms her nose in the length of his neck. "You are too good to me," she says, almost loud enough for him to hear.

Lili first met her husband in the casino of the Playa Beach Hotel in San Juan. His turquoise eyes and sunburned scalp stuck out more than the fingers he snapped to get her attention. She walked to him with her tray of free drinks, wobbling in high heels, wearing only a tuxedolike shirt that stopped at her blackstockinged thighs. Lili had gotten her job by sitting on a sofa and crossing her legs and finally by lifting her skirt and swirling it around, posing like the pictures she had seen of Marilyn Monroe. Her mother lay in bed with strange stomach pains and her father worked most of the year as a super in a Brooklyn apartment building. On weekends, Lili would go home to Ponce and lay her tips aside for the pills that soon lined every bathroom shelf. Her family told everyone she was in hotel management.

Billy Bluestone's hair was slicked straight back in a crewcut and the skin on his nose was flaky. He was an art dealer from Manhattan; he balanced his business card in the creases of his palm. Lili liked the sureness of his voice, the way he gestured with his nose and snapped his wrists back when he spoke Spanish but switched to English to curse at the dice and count his chips. Lili decided that, even if he was bowlegged and ten years older, it didn't matter. In the dark, walking on the beach behind the hotel, she saw only that his footprints in the sand engulfed her tiny steps.

He told her he always kept both feet on the ground and always made the right decisions. About business. About people. About her.

"You know about the three pigs?" he asked. "I'm the one built the house of bricks."

One night, Lili took him to the fishing village of La Parguera for a ride across Phosphorescent Bay. Captain Jack rode in circles until the movement of the boat's motor made little flashes of light appear in the water. He scooped up a bucket of dinoflagellates, poured them on deck, and they lit up like Christmas lights. Billy draped his jacket around Lili's shoulders and pointed out the stars in the Big Dipper. He said they looked close enough to touch and asked her which one she wanted.

Later, over dinner, he said to her, "When I was growing up in Brooklyn, we always had a piano in our apartment. Nobody ever played it in my family, but my mother dusted it every day and had it tuned twice a year. Nobody touched it, but it was important for my mother to keep that piano. I could tell it made her feel good just to see it there. And we moved a lot. Every time the rooms got a little shabby looking and the cracks came up over the radiators, we moved to another building. That way, we got a free paint job. And we moved that piano from apartment to apartment. It had to be lifted right through the kitchen window. I'd lean my head out and wonder what would happen if the rope slipped and the piano fell, but it never did." Billy Bluestone stared so hard at Lili, she blew air from her lips so he blinked.

"I'll get you a piano, Lili. If you marry me, I'll get you anything you want. I'll make you happy and I'll always come home."

Billy Bluestone squeezed her knee under the table. Lili knew she didn't love him, but with time she hoped she'd come close.

Lili takes a bus to Hato Rey, to the Hiram Bithorn Stadium, where the Santurce Crabbers play baseball from October to February. On the trip there, Lili sits closest to the driver and waves a dollar out the window at the men selling pork rinds in the streets. She twirls her hair with sticky fingers and reads the sports section of the *San Juan Star.*

At the stadium, Lili sells sodas and *tostones* and, when business is slow, she leaves the snack bar, winks at the guards, and sits in the *palcos*, the expensive five-dollar seats behind home plate. She watches women in tight black skirts and T-shirts lean over the fence and drop their phone numbers into the dugout.

I could never do that, Lili thinks. *I'd fall right over.* Once, for a week, she ate only peanuts and tequila until, with her blouse tucked tightly into spandex pants, Igor flirted with her in the market. He said she looked like a young Vanessa del Rio, the actress from the porno movies. That night, Billy Bluestone stopped at Marco's Panaderia y Reposteria and bought Lili coconut cookies, so sweet and rich that he licked each one of her

JANICE LEVY

fingers after she finished the box.

But even still, Lili thinks, she would not lean over the dugout and let the ballplayers look down her shirt. She is a married woman, *decente*, and prays every night to remain that way because her thoughts are all over the place. Sometimes, Lili sweats at night, as if drenched by a bucket of water. Sometimes, too, her toes tingle as if electricity were running down her legs. But worst of all is the crying, the tears spurting down her face without warning, like a sudden tropical storm.

When the games are over, Lili picks out the largest *surrullitos* left on the grill. She heats the cheese-filled corn sticks and packs them gently in a paper bag. Then she slips past the fans waiting for autographs outside the Cueva de los Cangrejeros and leaves the stadium.

On her way to the bus stop, Lili passes the players' parking lot. She spots the blue Mitsubishi with dark, smoky windows, license plate DJDJDJ. Lili knows the doors are never locked. She lays the *surrullitos* wrapped in a blue paper napkin on the driver's seat. She places the napkin faceup so Dickie Jon will see the kiss she has made with her red lipstick.

Blue Paper Napkin

When Lili gets home she watches the *noticias* and cooks *asopao*, dipping her fingers in the rice stew, tasting pieces of chicken as she stirs. Lili hears Dickie Jon tell reporters he was beaned in the head when he played for the New York Yankees two years ago, how he suffered from double vision. When he speaks Spanish, his voice deepens and hesitates; he uses only the present tense. He chews his moustache and scratches under his chin.

Lili licks her spoon. She wonders if his kisses could turn her inside out with their sweetness, if his hands would leave marks on her body. Lili imagines herself floating over center field, shadowing Dickie Jon's body with her silver nightgown, like a cloud clinging to a full moon.

When Billy Bluestone is out of town on business, Lili wakes up early, afraid to get out of bed, worrying that something terrible will happen to her if she goes farther than the porch. She counts the steps it takes to get to the kitchen, how many giant steps she needs to cross the living room. The smell of laundry detergent makes her head pound and she can't decide which color socks to hang first on the clothesline. Before Lili leaves for work, she looks in the mirror and imagines her skin turning as rough as a saddle, the bags under her eyes drooping enough to carry coins. As she walks to the bus stop, she can feel her knees sagging, imaginary claws of gravity pulling her closer to the ground. She knows that men look at her still, but more with a raised eyebrow than with a swivel of the neck and pursed lips.

At the ballpark, Lili keeps a radio behind the snack counter and raises the volume when the crowd yells, "Dickie, Dickie." Even with her eyes closed, she can see him swing. She knows that first he will rub dirt between his hands, then hitch up his pants from the back, pat his zipper, and spit, always toward first base. Then he will take three practice swings and cross himself quickly before he gets in the batter's box. If he calls time and steps out

JANICE LEVY

of the box, scowling, she knows he will lay down a bunt.

When Billy Bluestone comes home from a business trip, Lili rents the movie *Vaselina* and they kiss when John Travolta and Olivia Newton-John embrace. Then she lights red candles, piles her hair on her head, and moves her hips to Chayanne's "Provocame" until beads of sweat break out above Billy's lips.

Billy picks another anniversary to celebrate: the first day they met, the day they first kissed, the night he proposed, the time she accepted. They walk through the Plaza de San Jose and sit on the bench under the statue of Ponce de León. Billy kneels and the pigeons peck at the birdseed in his open palm, then sit on his shoes and shoulders. They climb a steep hill to the Iglesia de San Jose, and Billy asks if she remembers their wedding, the way the tourists stood in the open doorspace of the church and snapped pictures. He jokes that her beautiful face is on the wall of houses all over the world. "They can only look. I've got the real thing," he says.

Lili holds him from behind as they watch some old men play dominos under a gazebo. Billy whispers that the man with the beige Panama hat is cheating, the numbers he scribbles with a broken pencil point squeezed between his fingers are incorrect. Lili hugs her husband so hard that he groans. She rubs her wet face against the back of his shirt.

They drive to the *mundillo* shops of Aguadilla and walk hand in hand through Maria Lassalle's tiny store of linens and laces. Lili touches the rows of handmade *mundillos* wound on cards. Billy Bluestone fingers an infant's crib cover, with embroidered leaves in satin stitches and a three-inch *mundillo* border. Lili pretends not to see him wink. Billy slaps his wallet on the counter for the three dresses and matching handkerchiefs he has insisted she buy.

The seamstress stops stitching from the wooden box frame on

Blue Paper Napkin

her lap. "*Que suerte,*" she whispers, congratulating Lili on her luck. "Soon you'll come back for these." She holds up a pair of lace-edged bloomers with yellow duck appliqués.

When Billy Bluestone is home, Lili turns into an antenna. She can hear past his voice, through his laughter, underneath the noise. She makes his drink before he asks; she can hear his saliva rebounding off his throat. She hears his brain twitch, like the jump start of a car, and knows when he has something important to say. When one day he complains of chest pain, Lili isn't surprised. She can hear a double beat.

Lili tells no one of her new powers. When she goes to the ballpark, she dabs perfume on the inside of her thighs and outlines her mouth with red pencil. She is scared only by the sound of her own hunger.

The last day of the season, Lili stays late to clean the inside of the refrigerator and scrape the top of the grill. By the time she leaves the stadium, holding her *surrullitos* wrapped in a blue paper napkin, the parking lots are empty. Lili walks toward the bus stop, hurrying to get there before it gets dark.

"Hey, don't you work—" Lili jumps as a horn beeps. Dickie Jon pulls his car alongside and rolls down his window.

"At the snack bar. Your uniform," he yells over pounding rap music.

Lili nods and smiles and swallows at the same time. She curls her hair behind her ear and inhales sharply.

Dickie Jon leans across the front seat and pushes the door open. "Where you goin'? Give you a ride. Gonna rain any second, don't it look it? C'mon."

Lili hesitates, her hair blowing in her eyes, across her face, sticking to her lipstick. She fingers the side seams of her uniform.

"You know who I am?" he asks, tilting his head, his smile full of straight, white teeth. "Get in."

JANICE LEVY

As Lili closes the car door behind her and straightens her skirt, she drops the blue paper napkin with the red kisses onto the mat.

Dickie Jon's mouth forms an O and he blushes. Lili catches her breath and hears thunder.

Dickie Jon pulls the car off the road and parks under a tree. His eyes travel past her face to her fingers pinching the crook of her elbows. "So you're—"

"Yes. You?"

"Was."

"Any—"

"A boy. D.J.'s three. You?"

Lili spreads out her palms.

"Once she brought him out. Kid watched batting practice, ate a hot dog, and fell asleep. She don't let me see him much."

Dickie Jon rubs his chin and Lili notices a white scar under his lower lip. Without thinking, she touches it with her fingernail, then draws back suddenly.

"My old man. He popped me one. 'Cept he forgot to take his ring off."

Lili lifts her hair off her neck and points to a mark under her earlobe.

"Mine, too."

It is there that Dickie Jon kisses her first.

"You should tell me to stop," he says.

"Stop."

Lili makes a handprint on the fogged-up window and feels the heat in the car. When he kisses her between the eyebrows, it is hotter still. *I dreamed you*, she thinks but doesn't say.

"Me, too," he whispers into her neck.

Dickie Jon doesn't close his eyes as he unbuttons the collar of her blouse or as he tugs at his belt. Before he kisses her lips, he pauses. Lili hears the *coqui, coqui* of tiny frogs as the rain comes down hard against the windows.

"Damn frogs," he laughs. His breath smells of *sofrito* and

Blue Paper Napkin

oranges.

"*Está bien*," she hears a voice in her head. "It's okay," it says again and Lili covers his lips with her own.

Lili does not remember getting off the bus, does not remember which key finally opens up her front door. She spends the next few hours waking, sleeping, shivering, sweating. She feels Dickie Jon all over her, as if he were bath oil she had rubbed into her skin.

When Billy Bluestone comes home, she listens to his day at the gallery, fading in and out among details, then complains of a bad headache. Billy props up the pillows and puts a cool towel to her head. He brings a tray of coffee and *pan dulce* with jelly and sits on the edge of the bed. "Mind if I turn on the TV?" he asks, then turns the channel to the ten o'clock news.

"There's your place again," Billy says. "How many home runs you hit today?"

Lili sits up suddenly as she sees Dickie Jon being interviewed in the locker room. A reporter congratulates him on leading the Crabbers in RBIs and stolen bases. He wishes him luck in the major leagues and asks if he thinks the Yankees are worried about his double vision returning. Dickie Jon shakes his head and laughs. "Look what they said about Elvis. 'You ain't goin' nowhere, son. You ought to go back to drivin' a truck.' The Grand Ole Opry fired Elvis after one show." Dickie Jon stuffs a wad of tobacco in his cheek. "I plan on making New York my home for the rest of my life."

Dickie Jon hitches his pants, pats his zipper, and smiles.

Lili runs into the bathroom. She stays under the shower until the knocking on the door stops, until the steam rises from her body, like the soul of a wounded volcano.

"What is it?" Billy Bluestone asks again.

Lili shrugs and shakes her head, pulling her fingers so her

JANICE LEVY

knuckles crack.

"Tell me how to make you happy. Tell me what to do," he says.

Lili moves her mouth like a baby bird, but no sound comes out. When she finally speaks, it is to herself, in a voice that sounds rusty and stiff. "Us," she says, quieting the hiss of the *s* with her fingers. Then she raises her arms and hides from his turquoise eyes.

Billy Bluestone clears his throat and taps his teeth with a pen. He talks quickly and tucks in his shirt.

"We'll go away. Take a vacation. Go someplace. Wherever you want. I'll take some time off. Any place where I get to look at my beautiful wife and tell her how much I love her."

"Yes," Lili hears herself say. "That will be good. Would you like some coffee?" She squints and smiles distantly, as if posing for a picture on a baseball card.

Later, when she has gone to bed, she hears a noise coming from the kitchen. Billy Bluestone weeps like a baby goat, his face open, hiding nothing.

Lili thinks suddenly of being five, maybe six, and her father crying in the kitchen, of breaking glass, and a chair being thrown. She remembers how his hands shook, how his fingers looked like frightened worms, crawling shadows on the table under the glare of the bare lightbulb.

"Don't!" Her mother had run out of the room, covering her eyes. "Don't you do this to me!"

Lili touches the back of Billy Bluestone's head, wipes his tears with her thumbs. She wonders what she owes to a man she has seen weep.

Later that night, Lili takes Billy Bluestone's fingers to where she was touched before, moving his hips gently to a new song.

"Show me, Lili," Billy whispers. "Please. I love you."

Blue Paper Napkin

"I love you, too," she says and means it.

Lili makes love to the man she married when her legs were so slim they reached up to the sky, when she thought time was as open-ended as the sea.

Then she starts to erase Dickie Jon, bit by bit, until he is no bigger than a pair of lips on a blue paper napkin.

Christine Turner
Improvisational comedian

Interview
by Linda Davies

Christine Turner is a comedian who's worked Portland for the last ten years. One of the founders of the improv comedy group Brainwaves and, most recently, the Raging Hormones, she is ready for another adventure. By the time this issue is out, Christine will know what it's like to live and work comedy in New York City.

Prior to the interview, I'd asked Christine for some background material, which she generously provided. So when I arrived at her apartment, I already knew quite a bit about this master of improvisation.

Christine Turner

DAVIES: *As a preschooler, you spent time in South Africa and in Puerto Rico and learned both Swahili and Spanish. What do you remember of that?*
TURNER: I don't remember any Swahili whatsoever. What I do remember about both of those places was feeling isolated. We lived for a while in Durban, South Africa, a regular-size city, but we spent a lot of time on the road because my father was practicing his specialty of parasitology so we had to go out into

Improvisational comedian

wherever the wilderness is in South Africa. We weren't around city folk, and we weren't around people who spoke English, and we weren't around any other white people. I remember that feeling also, in Puerto Rico, when I was surrounded only by Spanish-speaking children—craving acceptance, even knowing it was going to be fleeting, that there would be another place coming up.

Communication has always been important to me. My mother argues with me about this, but I swear to God my first memory was—she says it must have been when I was between twelve and sixteen months—I remember watching my mother and her mother, my grandmother, whom we hardly ever saw, sitting in chairs talking. I was sitting on the floor. I have this memory of knowing they were doing something that was bringing them close together and that *I* couldn't do it.

I think that learning how to read early and being very verbal was all part of that wanting to participate and to hear other voices. Reading a book when I was a child, and still, as an adult, is like having a conversation with somebody I would never get to meet, a way of making a connection with somebody I would never ever have the opportunity to sit down and talk with. I don't know what that has to do with that whole Swahili Puerto Rico thing, but anyway.

In what ways are we permanently bound to or by our families?

I wish I knew. I do know that much of my comic sensibility, my perspective, the words I use, have to do with my family and the way we interacted with each other. So, even though I'm very far away—my family all lives in Los Angeles now—if you put all my siblings and me in the same room, we would immediately start talking the same language. Although none of the others is a performer, they are all very funny, very sarcastic. That was something that we all did as children: who could be the most entertaining, who could make the other people laugh. Whoever was the funniest was the one in control. I still have that impulse,

Interview: CHRISTINE TURNER

so do my brothers, although I don't know if my brothers would acknowledge it as such.

So, I think that even if you try to burn your bridges with your family, they live within you. I know that for most women their worst nightmare is growing up and becoming their mothers. That is definitely true for myself, although there are a lot of things I like about my mother. And yet the older I get, the more I sound like her, the more I find myself getting kind of eccentric like she is. I resist it, but I think those seeds were planted a long time ago. I also wonder if some of it isn't genetic.

The materials you sent—

Ah-ha! The pages and pages of tortured writing. Oh, my God.

How many hours did it take and how did you feel when you were done?

I felt a sense of accomplishment. This was the first time I'd ever done that from beginning to end, writing down what I thought were some of the important times of my life. And then, once I'd sent them to you, I felt extremely embarrassed.

Overexposed?

It wasn't that so much. I don't really care if people know what's happened to me. The thing, I think, that made me feel self-conscious was thinking about what it looked like to somebody who didn't know me. It seemed kind of self-indulgent and reckless and uncontrolled, as if I were on some sort of binge. Usually, I'm very careful about presenting things in a way that will be palatable and people can take it because I'm going to make it very funny for them. Although it might make them uncomfortable, I'll dress it up with enough jokes and then they'll be able to swallow it. When I was writing *that* [background materials], I didn't do that at all. I wasn't funny and I was truthful and I wasn't sure if it would scare you, or make you feel all weird, like: *I'm not going over there. She's crazy.*

No. It felt very bold and unprotected. It reflects a fair amount of courage to do that, in my estimation.

Improvisational comedian

You wrote about going through life pretty comfortably until you changed neighborhoods and schools in the sixth grade. You said a heck of a set of words: "These were the events that turned me into a tortured, misunderstood artist and attention slut." If you had said that to me in person, I expect it would have been framed as a joke, but I had the feeling that you fully meant it.

Oh, I did. Even when I'm joking, I usually mean everything I say.

I was afraid of that. How do you suppose that whole thing happened?

You know, I'm not really sure. It's the first thing I can remember happening to me individually outside of my family, that I had to deal with myself. It was so unexpected. I'd gone from being this perfect kid at the old school where they thought I was amazingly bright: Here comes this person into kindergarten, who can read on a sixth-grade level and, in the first grade, can read on a college level. The teachers thought this was great and I got a lot of praise. I was also very athletic. Sometimes I wonder if I've mythologized it, because it seems like everything was fine.

And there was a series of events that happened outside of school, too. I had a grandmother who died—a grandmother with whom I was very close, who gave me books and was really sort of my special person. And the Manson murders, which was a huge, terrifying thing for me. I was absolutely paranoid that I was going to be murdered.

How old were you then?

I was ten. That was the beginning of the anxiety. I never said anything to my parents, although I sort of hinted to them. When we moved, I said, "Is this going to be a bigger city or a smaller city?"

My mother, thinking she was going to be comforting me, said, "Oh, it's a smaller city."

Well, then I was even more terrified because a smaller city meant my chances of being murdered were even greater. The

Interview: CHRISTINE TURNER

whole idea of random killings—this is what drove me crazy about the Manson family murders—that they would just arbitrarily pick somebody, and I was sure that it was going to be me and I was going to be stabbed to death.

This was a fixation for many years. Later, when I told my mother about this, she asked me why I hadn't said anything about it. It was like I knew it was crazy. Part of me knew it was irrational and I was afraid of letting anybody know what I was experiencing.

But then, when we finally got to the new school and this open hostility and the kind of cruelty that's legendary with kids, but was so unexpected for me, I think that it all came together into one internal experience, and I got rid of the old Christine and built up a new one who could take it. It was very calculated. I remember having that moment where I realized that I couldn't get away and I was going to have to find a way of coping. I constructed this extremely aggressive, razor-sharp, sarcastic, cruel humor. I became a frightening person, a bully, in a sense. I was completely out of control. I didn't know how to stop. I had to get fiercer and fiercer. I was in survival mode and created this monster in order to cope. It became bigger than myself.

I guess people will want to know what happened at school.

Well, it wasn't anything major. Nobody beat me up. Nobody degraded me in a really outrageous way. I came to this new school, and I became the target for everybody. I don't know if it was because I was the new girl. I don't know if it was because I was a little bit overweight at the time. I don't know if it was because it was the middle of the year. But the girls were constantly leaving me out and mocking me during recess and telling me I could be their friend if I would just do this or that. I remember, they told me I had to go around and tell everybody I was a homo. I didn't even know what that meant, but I spent the whole lunchtime going, "Hi, I'm Christine, a homo." Looking back, it's kind of funny.

Improvisational comedian

It was very cruel.

It was. I mean, for fifth-grade girls—I just had no experience with this. In the school where I had been before we had known each other throughout, from kindergarten through fifth grade. Whenever there were new kids—there were maybe one or two each year—this sounds really sentimental, but everybody was *nice* to them. We would all go out at recess and play baseball. We would divide up into teams and when people got up to bat and were afraid to swing, we didn't mock them or anything. We cut them some slack.

This was so intense and so mean and, for some reason, it was me. I didn't know what it was about me that could provoke such enmity.

And you thought it was something about you.

Yes, well, they weren't doing it to anybody else.

You were the only new kid?

My brothers were all new in the school and they had assimilated right away. Again, it was the first example for me in a long string of examples of being somehow different from the rest of my family. I did not fit in. I was a black sheep. I always felt this pressure from my family—*Please, can't you hide whatever it is you do, whatever that thing is, that antenna that goes up so people can tell you're different, you're weird? Can't you just pack it down?* That was when I chose to protect myself. If it came down to either getting an A for my family or protecting myself as a person, I opted for myself. That was the first time, but it became the thing that I did. I learned to trust my instinct.

That's one of the most valuable things a person has.

It is, but I think so many of us learn to stifle that, to conform and to believe that other people know what's best for us. To buck the system is a very scary thing, even when everything in your gut tells you you can't go their way. When my parents' marriage was breaking up and it was really awful at home and I was in that house-bound thing, where I didn't leave the house

Interview: CHRISTINE TURNER

for two years—I realized I did not want to end up like my parents.

They had done everything right. They had goals. If this is how it all turns out, forget it! I'd rather be living in poverty, which is what I do compared to the rest of my family. How I live scares the hell out of them, but the way they live scares the hell out of me—never really connecting with anybody, always afraid to say the truth because you might lose something or somebody might know something about you and use it against you later.

But, you know, I'm also afraid I'll end up in some flophouse, eating cat food, watching soap operas and afraid to leave my apartment because somebody might take my Social Security check. There are no guarantees. I wish there were guarantees, but there aren't.

No, there aren't. Suppose you'd never left your original neighborhood, that you'd stayed in that safe place, what would your life be like now?

I haven't really thought about that, but I think it would have been pretty much a straight course and I would have been the neighborhood girl who went off to college and the neighborhood girl who did well.

At fourteen you ran off with your eighteen-year-old girlfriend. It sounds like that was a rough period.

It was. It was like nothing I have ever seen or done since. This is how naive I was: I had just turned fifteen. My father had sent me on this sort of rehab trip during the summer to Idaho with some other kids—boys—my age, who were in this therapy group I was in. I started plotting to run away because I knew when I came back I was going to be forced to go to school and my father was going to be in Europe and I was going to have to live with my mom, and I just didn't want to do it. I was reading a magazine on the bus and it said there was this lesbian commune in Georgia. I thought, *Okay, let's just go there. All you have to do is go to Georgia and ask where the lesbian commune is and they'd point and you'd get there and they'd welcome you with open arms.*

Abby and I ended up getting a ride to Georgia from this man who said he was going to visit his family. Two days later, they threw him off the farm and we had no place to stay. Within half an hour of being dropped off, the whole town knew we were there. We were from California, so they thought that we were prostitutes and that we had been brought there by this very rich man for sexual purposes. But we didn't know they thought this. In a way it was kind of a joke, this whole mistaken identity thing. It was so hard to know what was going on and who to trust. People would one minute come up to us and offer us a place to stay for the night, and the next day they wouldn't talk to us at all. They'd pretend we weren't there.

And it was very racist. I once had someone come up to me and warn me because I went into a convenience store and a young black man said hi. I said hi back to him, and I was told in the store—by a complete stranger—"You better not be seen talking to a nigger or people are going to get the wrong idea." I could not believe it. This was in 1974. I thought that was very strange.

A lot of really bad, scary things happened while we were there because we were runaways and we couldn't tell people we were runaways. We had a sexual relationship at the time and we couldn't tell people about that. We were both extremely vulnerable.

Through all of this, somehow we were physically unharmed. But there were a lot of times when guns were pulled on us and men attempted to sexually assault us. Again, it was an instinct thing—knowing who was cool and who wasn't, if this was going to be a dangerous situation or if it wasn't, how much I could talk my way out of and how much I couldn't. After about four months, though, I felt desperate to get out of there. I felt I could only bluff for so long. It was a matter of time before someone was going to rape me, hurt me, or kill me. As people began to discover that I was a runaway, I realized that they knew

Interview: CHRISTINE TURNER

they could make me disappear and nobody would know.

There were a few people who were really nice to us and took care of us and looked out for us. They went out of their way to help us, even though they didn't know us from Adam.

You were children, really.

Yeah. It was extremely stressful. When I finally came back to California I was fifteen, but I'd go to a restaurant and people would offer me drinks, and I thought, *I look way older now because I've been through hell.*

Is there something that you took from that whole experience that you feel is valuable to you?

What I learned was that, if I had to, I could live by my wits.

You said that people sometimes call you Bette Davis, suggesting that you're overly dramatic. How do you respond to that?

Early on, it used to really piss me off. "Oh, Christine, you're just being melodramatic," meaning I was overreacting and my version of events was not true. It was embellished, exaggerated.

Later on, I think I *would* put on, in a sense, a show. I would tell stories in a way that people stopped and listened. I would act out the parts and do voices and be kind of loud and entertaining. People would praise me, saying that I was entertaining to watch and to be around: "You should do something with that. You're such an actress, why don't you go into drama? Why don't you become a comedian?" And I would think, *Oh no. I couldn't do that. I can do* this, *but I couldn't do that.* I didn't even understand that there was a connection between the two things.

Please finish this sentence: Most people are basically _____.

Afraid.

What is the difference between humor and comedy?

I think that humor can be a passive thing. Having a sense of humor means that you can see a funny side to things. Something humorous may be unintentional. Something might happen and it wasn't set up to be funny, but it turned out to be. You saw it and it struck you as funny. That, to me, is humor. It doesn't have anything to do with performing or making something happen. It's kind of a natural thing. People either have a sense of humor or they don't. I don't know if you've ever met people who don't have a sense of humor. I don't know where they come from or what their story is, but they are pieces of work, to be sure.

Comedy is more of an intentional thing. It's taking something that's happened and figuring out the funniest way of telling it. Not necessarily veering away from the truth, but finding an order to the story where people can't see what's coming. The best comedy is where you can't see where it's going to end up. People are just along for the ride and then, boom, something happens and they find themselves surprised and delighted, and you were the one who took them on that trip. These people have trusted me to be their tour guide. That, to me, is what a show is about.

The funny thing about being a comedian is that, now, after living a life where I felt I had made a series of choices where a large segment of society was going to disapprove of me, I'm on stage in front of those same people. I take them somewhere that they can't get to on their own. Before a show, they see this goofy-looking fat girl and I don't strike any chord in them whatsoever. And then, after a show, people who I would think would be my natural enemies are saying, "Wow! You cracked me up."

An interesting turn of the tables.

Yes. And it amazes and delights me that I can get away with it. I am in their faces. Not only do they have to look at me, these people who didn't want to look at me for most of my life, but they will *pay* to look at me and they will laugh at my jokes, which are all about what idiots I think they are sometimes. I don't really have a hostile sense of humor, but all of this is born out of my experience of being denied access to their circle. Now they're paying to hear me regurgitate it. It is very bizarre. I don't get it. I don't get how it happened.

Interview: CHRISTINE TURNER

I remember doing a show for the Oregon Medical Association at this fancy hotel in Eugene. I was up on stage making this joke about OHSU [Oregon Health Sciences University]—and there was this big brouhaha about OHSU and Emanuel Hospital, some donor program. They were telling me to be very careful because the doctors were divided on issues about the program and it was a big controversial thing in the OMA at that time.

I set up this whole scene where people were coming to get organs. The organs were all in a tank, and I told them to pick one out, as they would a lobster for dinner. I went way over the edge on that. At first, there was a hush, and then people started laughing hysterically. These were all tuxedoed doctors—like my father—laughing helplessly. Afterward, doctors were coming up to me saying, "Oh, you are so talented." I couldn't believe it. They were talking to me; they were talking to me. They spent an hour in a room watching me pick ideas out of my head. To me, it was so gratifying. I felt as if I had won.

When I watch you work, you are right in people's faces, but I've never seen you be mean. What do you generally think about your audiences? You seem to have a little bit of room for them.

I usually just love the audience. I'll do anything for the audience. There are those isolated incidents, like at the corporate shows where I get a weird, disoriented feeling because I'm working in front of people who, in real life, have so much more power and prestige than I do. For that hour, I own them in a sense, because they're watching me. They could never do what I'm doing, and what I'm doing terrifies them. If you talk to them in the audience, all of a sudden they don't know what to do, they're so nervous. It's that turning-the-tables thing I really like. Although I'm never mean to them; it's a personal thing in my mind.

Audiences have varied from place to place. When I really started honing my craft at the Embers, there was a huge gay boy audience. I found a good home there with them because they didn't have the kinds of attitudes about women that I encountered with straight men. So, it was like: *You go, girl.* Anything I wanted to do, they didn't care. I could get vulgar. I could be sexual. I could step over the line and do things that weren't ladylike. I could play male characters. They just thought it was great, as long as I was funny. They really supported all the early character work; they'd come back to see my characters week after week. That gave me a lot of confidence and also made me feel really accepted. I could experiment and feel that the audience was on my side.

I thought for a long time that I didn't like having straight men in the audience. But then as we traveled around in Brainwaves to these little redneck towns—we've been to some really redneck towns—I found that I was able to make them laugh, too, and that they would bend the rules for me. Sometimes they would heckle me at the beginning and I would say something back, and then they'd say, "Guess she told you, Sam! Heh, heh, heh." It would be like a pissing contest at first, but once I'd established that I was going to be up there and I was going to do it and it didn't matter what they thought, then all of a sudden they were my big fans. These guys with cowboy hats, these little shitkickers from Idaho, Wyoming, and Montana, and stuff, who'd never seen improv and never seen a woman on stage ever in their life. At the beginning of a show I'd think, *Oh, forget it*—but I found myself connecting with them, too.

I bet that changes both you and them.

It does. I don't know what happens to them in the rest of their lives, but I've found that I'm as judgmental as I fear other people to be with me. I found myself reacting to what I perceived as instant rejection from them—that they would never accept me, would never listen to anything I had to say. I wasn't pretty enough to hold their attention, so it wasn't going to work. Most of the time I'm proved wrong. I walk away thinking, *Hmm, I had that all wrong.* If you make them laugh, they'll forgive you

Interview: CHRISTINE TURNER

anything.
All the stereotypes go to hell.
They really do. If somebody feels like you respect them while you're making them laugh, a unique relationship develops. My favorite shows happen when I feel as though the audience and I are almost breathing at the same time. I can remember a few shows when I would come on stage after being off for a minute and I would hear this whisper of excitement going, "Oh, there she is again! I wonder what she's going to do." And I felt like I could talk to the audience almost as one person. There was no anxiety. There was no pushing at it. It just flowed in and out, just as easily as breathing.

Those feelings—it's such a comedown after the show. You leave the stage and make your way through the bar or the auditorium, and those feelings are gone. It's weird.
What's it like being part of the Raging Hormones group?
Ah, it is the most fun that I've had since I started doing improv. Rita and Cindy are friends of mine, so there's a real personal aspect to it, and then there's the professional aspect for me after being in a different comedy group for a long period of time. Although I was a founding member of that comedy group and never felt the audience thought that the men were better than I was or that I played some secondary role, when we would go to clubs or when people would talk to us, they seemed to think that they should ask the guys what was going on. Even when a couple of us would have artistic disagreements, when it came right down to it, the guy's experience had been that he was the guy and he always won unless I was absolutely dogged about it. The fact of the matter is, except for exceptions like Roseanne, comedy is a very male-dominated business. I just got sick of it. After saying, "Well, I think this—" "Well, I don't—" "Well, I think this—" "Well, I don't—" for three days, finally I'd go, "Fine. Whatever."

Even when I worked with other groups, I found that whole

thing. There was always a guy who had to be in charge. There was always a guy who thought his stuff was funnier. And whenever they would write a sketch—you see it on *Saturday Night Live* all the time, too—there would be a female character who didn't have anything to do, really.

A supporting person.

Yeah. And the men got to do all the fun stuff and they never thought the women's sketches were as funny. You find that all the time within professional comedy groups. They have women in there because they need women, but it might be five men and one woman, six men and two women. I think a lot of men really believe that women are not as funny as men. And I think that Roseanne is a perfect case of the kind of backlash where—she's one of my heroes, you know—she's crucified for everything that she does. People resent the fact that she is funny so they make fat jokes about her. They're always trying to take away her power, trying to chip away at it and prove that she's just an unhappy person or that it just doesn't seem right for women to go balls to the wall like that.

One of my favorite things has been being on stage for the women in the audience. I always think about that whenever I go to a show. I don't care if the whole audience is women and there aren't any men there. People will say that to me, "Well, God, you sure draw a lot of women, don't you?"—as if there's something wrong with that, or it's not going to be that good of a show. I'm not sure what it is they're attaching to that, you know. So what. It's great. I like it. I love hearing women laugh and I know that they're seeing something that they don't usually get to see. And I know how empowering it is. When I saw Peggy Platt when I was twenty-five, before I started doing any comedy, and I saw her on stage, standing up there in that room full of people—and she was a fat woman, my age, up there making jokes—I thought, *That could be me!* There is so much people haven't heard from women. Women have to do all the tampon

Interview: CHRISTINE TURNER

jokes and the PMS jokes and the my-tits-are-so-small jokes and the my-butt-is-so-big jokes—all that stuff where they take away their own power. They just strip it away as a sort of entertainment. I don't think many women choose to do that, but it's one of the only things that they've been allowed to do on stage.

So working with all women is freeing in that way, because nobody gets assigned certain roles. Anybody can be whatever they want. We can all play the women; we can all play the men; we can all do whatever. We all have different histories and performing backgrounds. When we're really cooking together, I can feel all of us stretching in a way that we haven't done before. We have a lot of fun, and that's really important to me—to be having fun and the audience having fun—for it to be balanced. I've seen shows where the audience is kind of left out: *Okay, you shut up now and watch what we're going to do.* I don't really like that.

You prefer the inclusive.

Yes, I do.

I think the audience does, too. Do you have a favorite character?

I haven't done this one in a long time, but there used to be a character I was well known for in Brainwaves. Her name was Doris Beasley. The thing that I really liked about her was that she is the kind of person—I ride the bus all the time—she's like someone you'd meet on the bus, who would just start talking to the whole population on the bus. At first you'd think she was really crazy and just seemed to be jumping from subject to subject, but somehow, through the course of it, you could see what the connection was between each thing. I used to love doing that character because it was almost like I was channeling it. I never knew what I was going to say. I never knew how things were going to get tied up in the end, but they always seemed to, somehow. People loved that character so much that they started a fan club for her. The thing that I thought was so interesting about it was that this was someone everybody would turn away from during the day.

Improvisational comedian

What is the nature of that?

I don't know. The first time I did my monologue I thought, *Oh God, everything's coming through that everybody hates. They're going to turn away. This is too intense, too true, too gross.* Instead, they'd go in. It's that peculiar thing about art. If you were waiting for the bus and this lady was talking to you, you'd be going, *Oh, God, will you shut up!* But yet people will sit transfixed and laugh and think that she's just the cutest thing in the world when she's on stage. And it's the same with me. I'll be walking down the street and somebody will drive by me and shout, "Hey, you fat piece of shit!" or whatever. And yet I know that if I was on stage, that same person would be pissing their pants with laughter. And I would not have changed at all. It's a weird thing. I don't really understand it. I just know it's true because I've been on both ends of it.

George Rabasa

I was hot and itchy in the charro suit; such was the price of looking macho.

George Rabasa's fiction has appeared in *StoryQuarterly*, *Other Voices*, *Side Show '94*, and *Stiller's Pond*, an anthology from the upper Midwest by New Rivers Press. A collection of his short stories is in search of a publisher.

Rabasa is a first-generation American of Hispanic descent, born in Maine, raised in Mexico City. For most of his life, he bounced back and forth between the two countries until the fates conspired, some ten years ago, to place him, more or less permanently, right in the middle of the exotic Midwest. George Rabasa lives in Minneapolis with his wife, Juanita, and two above-average cats.

GEORGE RABASA
The Beautiful Wife

In the time that it took to lift a glass of real champagne, acquired at a good price from a friend in the Mexican Consulate in San Diego, make a silent toast to her fifty-second wedding anniversary, and swallow the whole thing down, Doña Artemisa Valle decided that her husband had to go.

At that particular moment she had no idea where Don Carlos should be. Another building, another city, another country. The farther the better: Alaska. What could be farther and bleaker and more isolated than Alaska, for a Mexican?

She pictured him in an igloo, his short, pudgy body wrapped in bear fur, three days' growth of beard sprouting on his cheeks, his stiff, frostbitten fingers clutching the leather-bound notebook where he had been writing his memoirs every afternoon since moving from Mexico City to Santa Alma, California, twelve years ago.

She looked around the table at her daughter Carmen, at her son, Luis, at her husband, and was grateful that none of them could read minds. She held her glass out for her son to refill, and this time took only a couple of small, delicate sips. The bubbles tickled her nose and she burst out laughing. She was seventy years old and, contrary to expectations, she was enjoying life. If her husband chose to mope around, then he should do it someplace where his moods wouldn't affect everybody else's.

George Rabasa

Artemisa watched her husband pick at the cake, fastidiously separating the layers so that he could scrape away more of the cream filling with the edge of his fork. "But what are you doing, viejo?" she exclaimed. "You think an extra pound or two on that old carcass matters to me? Enjoy yourself, amor. It's our anniversary."

"It's too sweet," he shrugged.

"Too sweet," she mimicked him. "Too salty, too oily, too big, too this, too that. You have to enjoy life."

"I'm busy enough living," he said, "without the extra requirement of having to enjoy the process as well."

Everybody agreed that Artemisa looked younger and more beautiful than ever when she returned the night before from her latest trip to Dr. Illhoffer's famous Living Cells Clinic in Ellesberg, Switzerland. Even with the flight to San Diego arriving hours late, and then the sleepy drive through the hills to Santa Alma, there was a special glow to Doña Artemisa's skin, still smooth and nutty brown and luminous, and the sparkle in her black eyes twinkling wherever she looked.

Her two children meeting her at the airport made her feel special. Waiting to give her big abrazos was Carmen, who had obtained permission from her convent in Los Angeles. Beside her stood Luis, who was her favorite because he had deep dark eyes just like hers. Missing was her youngest daughter, Marcela, who had broken her solemn promise to lead a moral life and therefore was banned from her mother's side.

Seeing her children had made Artemisa particularly happy because she had felt all alone on the long trip back from Geneva. What kind of company is a husband who laments constantly, and who already smells like an old man because his inner gases are seeping out of every pore in his body?

It was no wonder she had felt glad to be alone in her own separate room for the fourteen days' stay at Dr. Illhoffer's clinic, because Don Carlos was apt to ruin the good effects of the $7,500 injections of cells drawn from the vital organs of a freshly aborted lamb fetus, with his malingering and his negativity, and especially his sudden bursts of concupiscence, too odd in a man his age to be charming. Because, wouldn't you know it, right on the eve of receiving the first dosage of the Living Cells, when they were both supposed to be resting their bodies and their minds with meditation and a fruit-fast and a darkened room, the silly old man attained a sturdy erection, his first in months, and walked down the hallway to her room in the middle of the night. Of course, she couldn't deny him his pleasure. A wife has her duties. She managed nevertheless to keep a restful mind; as far as her husband was concerned, she was sure that the life of the lamb sacrificed for his benefit had been a total waste.

She was explaining all this to her daughter Carmen, Hermana Carmen in the convent, dressed in a high-buttoned blouse and a gray skirt that came down to her boxy lace-up shoes. Then turning to her son, Luis, all in black leather that still smelled pungently new, she hooked her arm in his and looked up at him with her sparkling, flirtatious eyes.

Luis had hired a limousine for the ride to Santa Alma. When Artemisa saw the cream-colored stretch driven by a good-looking Anglo in a blue military cap and a crisp white shirt, she insisted they take photos.

"Find a camera, one of those disposable ones," she said to Luis. "After all, I've been gone for two weeks, and I feel like a changed woman. Sí, Luisito, let's take pictures so we can remember when we're no longer as beautiful."

She unbuttoned her dark green silk coat to reveal a pale salmon blouse and a black leather skirt cut well above the knee. She held a small, square cosmetics bag that matched the rest of the six-piece red luggage set which the driver had lined up before her. She blew a kiss toward the group and waited for the click of the shutter. "Stand up straight," she coaxed Carlos. "Otherwise, people will realize that you are getting shorter and shorter with every passing year. I didn't marry a chaparro."

"Vieja," he said patiently. "We are both shrinking. It's the years. They start getting heavy."

"Speak for yourself," Artemisa said, pulling herself erect, placing her fists on her waist, and tilting her head back. "Shoot the picture, mi hijito," she told her son. "Finish the roll so that we can get them developed tomorrow. I want a record of this, the most vital night of my life."

In the mornings, Artemisa rises early, often while it's still dark. She has her coffee, thick and sweet and fragrant of cinnamon just like in Mexico, on the terrace of her eighteenth-floor condominium right on the coast. While her family sleeps, she enjoys the gradual unfolding of the fog that hides the ocean in the first few morning hours, the rising sun burning away the layers of mist to reveal the rocky shore, the secluded beaches, the rows of tall palms along the coastal highway that meanders north to San Juan Capistrano and Santa Barbara and Los Angeles.

The highway also leads south to Tijuana. But Artemisa does not like to think of the country they left twelve years before, traveling at night like gangsters in a big black car loaded down with money—dollars, not pesos—the three kids squabbling in the back seat, their parents up front, praying that the results of the surprise audit of the Procurement Office that Carlos ran would not be made public while they were still in Mexico. Not that Artemisa felt they had anything to be ashamed of. There were unwritten rules for government work, chief of which were that for six years you worked fourteen hours a day, seven days a week; you ruined your health with ritual drinking and rich food; and you watched your back for disgruntled leftists and greedy underlings. In exchange for that, you made your money. The fact that Carlos Valle had been singled out for an investigation was mainly a matter of unfortunate timing, the result of a suddenly bankrupt economy known as la crisis, which got fingers pointing in every direction. Now, with a two-story condominium in a building where they felt among friends because there were so many Mexicans living here that the compound was known as Taco Towers by jealous Anglos, and their nest egg locked away in a Grand Cayman trust, she was proud of Carlos.

Doña Artemisa was not one to brood for long; she had calls to make this morning.

"Querida," she said to her friend Sarita Bustamente, whose brother's construction firm had built most of the airports in Mexico. "You won't believe how wonderful the food was, and yet I lost at least ten pounds. They serve you tiny, tiny portions. But everything is so fresh! You can actually see them churning the butter in the village for your lunch the same day. How do I feel? I am so deliciously skinny you have to see me to believe it. It's a miracle. Carlitos? He is exactly the same as always."

George Rabasa

"Querida," she said to her friend Marta Galdós, who was the widow of a former head of Pemex, the oil company. "I am fine, but I am very worried about Carlitos. He is becoming a depressive. Some days I don't think I can handle it. All he did while we were in Switzerland was complain of being left alone in his room, about the food, the doctors, the language. Can you believe it? He actually told Dr. Illhoffer that they were a bunch of charlatans, that he wouldn't be taking the Living Cells if it weren't for me, and that in fact he was watching over me, lest I squander all our money on their voodoo treatments. Yes, I've been married to him for fifty-two years, but between his outbursts and then his moping, I don't know what to do with him."

"Querida," she said to her friend Doris Macías, who had been the special friend of the governor of Guanajuato way back when the exchange rate was twelve pesos and fifty centavitos for one U.S. dollar, instead of three thousand and something, like it is now. "I'm going to have to do something with this man. Carlitos is driving me crazy. He does nothing but fret about money. Of course, we have enough to get by, in a nice way, you understand. He is worried that the government is going to take it back from him. No, not the U.S., the Mexicans. Imagine such a thing."

Carlos Valle awoke to the sound of his wife's voice, the words muffled across the large living room and the hallway leading to his own room. But the rhythm of the voice, the happy, energetic cadence of the words, were a sign that his wife had been up for at least a couple of hours. The reward for the long night of wide-eyed sleeplessness was precisely these couple of hours of sweet slumber after his wife was up.

That morning he was relieved that he was no longer trying to push his way against the crowds in the Zurich airport, then squeezing himself into the crowded 747, where they rode coach at his insistence so they would not attract attention by sitting up front, and finally arguing about the validity of their immigration documents with a surly INS man who treated them like wetbacks.

The worst moment had happened in the small Zurich men's shop where Artemisa had taken him, insisting that a man of his position shouldn't go around with frayed cuffs and collars that curled up. Pinpoint ceiling lights cast a warm glow over the brass-edged mahogany counters on which a prim man with manicured nails displayed, as if they were jewels, a selection of silk ties, lizard-skin belts, and Sea Island cotton shirts. From across the way, Carlos became aware of a short, squat man with brown skin and black hair and a rippled neck who had been looking through a book of fabric swatches and was now staring insistently in his direction.

"Buenos días," he said when his eyes met Don Carlos's. Turning to Artemisa with a small bow, he added, "It is interesting how one can hear voices from Mexico anywhere in the world these days."

Carlos turned to nod politely at the man, before he was drawn by Artemisa into inspecting another stack of shirts the clerk had placed on the counter. "It is a small world," Carlos said with a slight shrug.

"And getting smaller every day," the man said affably. "Which part of Mexico are you from?"

"We are from near San Diego, California," Artemisa said coolly.

"Ah, yes, of course," the man said. "But before that, you lived in Mexico, no?"

"Mexico City," Don Carlos nodded. "But we have been in the U.S. many, many years."

"Since before la crisis?" The man smiled broadly, displaying two gold-capped incisors on either side of his mouth. "Or after."

"I think you should try a button-down collar for a change,"

George Rabasa

Artemisa said to her husband, putting her fingers over his wrist and pulling him slightly away from the stranger. "It would give you a more youthful look."

"I think the señor is certainly youthful," the stranger said. "Is this a good place to buy shirts?" he asked. "Would you say this is the best place in Europe? You seem to be very knowledgeable, señora," he said to Artemisa. "I myself just came in here today for the first time. The prices are high, especially if you think in terms of pesos."

"You pay for quality," Artemisa said.

"Easier if you have dollars, or better, francs," the man said with a small bow. "I think I'll shop around a little before I decide." Then, just as he was about to go out the door, he turned again to the couple and said apologetically, "Excuse me, I have been rude. My name is Miguel Guerrero." He stepped up to Carlos offering his hand.

"S-S-Suárez." Carlos felt a warm glow on his face. "José Suárez and my wife, Ana María."

"Mucho gusto," the man said. "I thought you looked familiar for a second," he added. "But no, I can't remember where we might have met."

Now, emerging from his dark bedroom into the brilliant morning light that came through the large expanse of glass facing the ocean, Don Carlos could not shake the feeling of dread that the man in the shirt shop had recognized him. As far as he could tell, the squat dark figure in the metallic brown polyester suit and the no-longer-so-fashionable flowered tie could be any one of a dozen men who had worked for the Ministry of Public Works back in the years when he was heading the Procurement Office.

"He looked like he was going to insult me," Carlos said to Artemisa, just like that, out of the blue, as if he meant to confuse her with his constant statements that seemed to come out of thin air.

"Who, mi amor? Who would want to insult the sweetest man in the world?"

"The man in Zurich," he said testily, as if she were playing games in spite of knowing exactly who he was talking about. "The Mexican who was making believe he was buying shirts."

"Your imagination," Artemisa sniffed. "He is just another bureaucrat with more greed than brains."

"I was nervous," Don Carlos murmured.

"You thought quickly and gave him a false name. We don't have an obligation to socialize with people just because they happen to be from Mexico."

"I'm scared even now," Don Carlos admitted. "You know the government has people like him looking into the affairs of some of us who left."

"Look out the window, tonto," Artemisa said, standing up from the table and pulling Carlos to the edge of the terrace. Below, the ocean glimmered in the bright sun, spotted with huge splashes of a blue deeper than the color of the whole, then fragmenting against the rock formations in brilliant crystalline explosions. "See that? You can gaze out your window and say to yourself that you own that ocean, and nobody will come up here to contradict you."

"It makes me queasy to look down," Carlos said, stepping back from the edge of the terrace.

In the afternoon, Don Carlos worked on his Memorias. He read from the first page of the notebook:

> *I was born in 1917. Nobody could have guessed at the time the evil I would later be capable of doing. From the first memories of my childhood, I felt myself to be singled out for great things, to be a humanitarian, a scientist, a man of letters. But when I moved to Santa Alma at the age of sixty-two, I had accomplished everything I think I was meant to*

GEORGE RABASA

accomplish in life; I was married to Artemisa; I was the father of Luisito, Carmen, and Marcela; I had seven suitcases full of one-hunded-dollar bills, several cashier's checks made out in different amounts to different banks, and hundreds of gold coins wrapped in newspaper so they wouldn't jingle. Only Artemisa knows for sure how much it came to. We left in the middle of the night, Artemisa and I driving a big Ford Galaxy, the kids in the back seat, the money in the trunk. The only thing I missed from Mexico City was my dog, Azabache, a tall Labrador with a lustrous black coat. We left the dog with a bowl of water, and the house with all the furniture and clothes in the closets and food in the refrigerator, in the name of my friend in the Ministry of Foreign Relations, who had issued diplomatic passports for the whole family. My friend, from what I hear, is still living in my big beautiful house in Coyoacán. I hope he took good care of Azabache.

Even as Don Carlos turned to the next page, he knew it was blank. In the several months since he had begun, he had been unable to write any further. The simple beginning seemed so conclusively to wrap up the story of his life that there just wasn't anything left to say. To fill the remaining three hundred pages with prevarications, excuses, and finally, apologies, seemed a waste of time. But still he sat every afternoon at his writing table and, for an hour or two, he waited. It was not a matter of not remembering. He could at any time close his eyes and see the details of his life in the Ministry of Public Works. The lengthy contracts for streetlights or park benches or public restrooms, though he knew the villages would remain dark, that the parks did not exist, that the poor would continue to shit in vacant lots. There were the daily brown envelopes, crammed so full the seams had to be bound up with tape to keep them from splitting and exuding wrinkled, oily currency all over his desk. The lengthy quality-inspection reports for bridges and dams and roads that had been proposed and actually designed but never built. Most even had names, such as the Benito Juárez Dam or the Hidalgo Highway, and they were all put in files along with the proof of their shadowy existence: proposals, blueprints, competitive bids, purchase orders, payment records, quality certification. The system had existed for decades.

The problem was not a faulty memory, but that the Memorias had to be true, a record of the death of his soul, a confession to be made public after his death. He could picture his family discovering the small leather-bound book tucked unobtrusively next to his cherished *Chronicles of Bernal Díaz*, the poetry of Sor Juana, the translations into Spanish of ancient Nahuatl texts. *Las Memorias de Don Carlos Valle*. His wife would destroy them. His son, Luis, would not understand the shame. Carmen would refuse to read them. Only Marcela would realize that what he needed was forgiveness.

Marcela was the bright one, but Artemisa had banished her from the family for breaking the promise she had made as a fourteen-year-old, that she would stay a virgin until she married. Artemisa had extracted the vow from the girls as they were leaving Mexico City, and unless Marcela and Carmen promised sexual abstinence until they married, she would turn the car around and drive them back to the house in Coyoacán, where they would be safe from poaching gringo men.

Once a year, Artemisa and the girls went to see Dr. Alonso, a gynecologist with an office just on the other side of the border in Tijuana. His main practice involved giving elderly women potent hormone shots not readily available on the U.S. side. Also, as a special service to the Valle family, once a year he verified Marcela's and Carmen's virginity.

Things had gone normally, Carlos later learned from Marcela, until two years ago when she was twenty-two and seeing a boyfriend, not an Anglo, but a fine Mexican fellow she had met in one of her classes at the law school. Dr. Alonso took a look at the reflection in his speculum and then, without a word to

Marcela, marched out to reveal the latest development to Doña Artemisa, who was, after all, the client who paid his substantial fee.

Artemisa gave Marcela a week to leave the house, but the young woman left that same night and moved right into the apartment of her friend, Gustavo Eloy. Carlos had tried to dissuade Artemisa, who insisted she was responsible for the children's morals. He loved Marcela more than his other children simply because he understood her best. Carmen, with her intoxication with Jesus and the Virgin and the saints constantly churning in her heart, seemed something exotic and a little pathological to him. Luisito, who at thirty-five was the oldest, was content to sleep all day and then spend his nights in bars where everyone showed off their leather outfits. Carlos had accepted that an interest in motorcycles was not all there was to his son's mysterious ways.

He closed the notebook and leaned back from the massive oak desk that reminded him of the study he had when he was a lawyer in private practice. The colors had been rich and brown, and the desk big enough to spread open the massive notary books that contained in fine, blue calligraphy the details of wills and testaments, transfers of property, corporations' bylaws. The big leather chair creaked as he reached for the phone.

"Marcelita."

"You're back, Papito," she said cheerfully. "Are you younger?"

Don Carlos chuckled. "Those things work better on your mother. She gets revitalized. I end up with little more than a sore butt."

"That's because you have no faith."

He pictured her smiling at him. "I had ten thousand dollars' worth of faith."

"I take it back," she said. "Es mucha fe."

"How are you, Marcelita?" he asked seriously. "Are you happy still?"

"Sí, Papá. Still happy."

"Good, you are the happiest of the family. Your sister has a very grim marriage to Jesus. Your brother is still sleeping. And your mother is happy only when she is talking or shopping."

"And you, Papá, how are you doing?"

"I've been better, Marcelita."

"You need to get out of the house."

"That's what your mother says, too."

"I'll pick you up tomorrow and we'll go have lunch by the beach."

"No, not the beach," he said. "It is too wide open. It gives me a lost feeling."

"Then our apartment."

"That would be better. You can send out for pizza."

"You remember," she laughed. "It's the specialty of the house."

Doña Artemisa lay awake most of the night. There was no way a woman could sleep in peace when down the hall she knew her husband was rattling his old bones around, turning this way and that inside his little dark room, his shrunken body swamped by the big silk pajamas.

They had been married so long that, even if they didn't speak about it, she knew what he was thinking during his endless nights. He was thinking that he was nothing more than a toad, hovering about in the shallow corner of some dark swamp, that he was no better than a fly settling its furry little legs down on a mountain of cow shit, that he was a worm burrowing deep into the loamy black earth of the fallow winter fields. All because of the six years he spent in the government. All because of her. Because she had not been happy with the small pickings of his legal practice, had looked around at the other women in their circle and wept at the thought of all the fine things they could buy abroad that she couldn't even afford to go look at.

George Rabasa

Throughout the years, they had both been aware of a solemn contract, certainly unwritten, even unspoken, yet binding from the day of the wedding: she would be the most beautiful wife the little man could possibly aspire to, and he would become wealthy.

Neither had counted on the fact that the bookish little lawyer had the intellect to solve problems and the skills to manage a huge bureaucracy, but not the ability to plunder. Some men had an ear for music, or a heart for poetry, or hands for surgery. But Carlos Valle had no stomach for larceny; when he began his tenure in the Procurement Office and his secret bank accounts started bulging as if dam gates had been opened, his first thought was that something was wrong with his bowels, perhaps an ulcer or colitis, pray to God nothing more serious than that. Through those six years, poor Don Carlitos could keep nothing down but boiled potatoes, jars of Gerber's baby food, and warm glasses of frothing milk to ease the raging acid that burned like serpents' tongues up to the back of his throat.

She felt it was to her husband's credit that in spite of this lack of natural ability, he kept spreading open his arms to receive the flood of suppliers' gifts, the kickbacks from contractors, the bribes from the army of quality inspectors that descended in his name to check every kilometer of highway, every foot of bridgework, every brick of warehouse construction that came under his domain. She could not forget that the little man had given up his health for her.

For the third time that night, she heard him carefully open the door to his bedroom and pad barefoot down the hall to the bathroom. She wondered how one small person could piss so much. She herself would never wake up at odd hours if it weren't for her husband's sleeplessness, which was as contagious as the flu.

"Are you all right, mi vida?" she called out from her bed.

"Yes, I'm fine," he said, peering into her dark bedroom. "I

The Beautiful Wife

didn't mean to wake you, querida."

"I've told you I can't sleep if you are having troubles."

"I am not having troubles," he insisted. "Just thoughts."

After a moment, seeing that he remained at her door, holding it open just enough to let in a sliver of light from the hallway, she added, "Are you going to stand there all night? Come to my bed for a little while, viejito."

He lay on his back beside her, very still, their bodies not quite touching but close enough for him to feel the warmth of her flesh, the scent on her skin, the slight rise and fall of the blanket along with her breathing.

"Why can't you be happy, Carlitos?" she murmured so softly he was not sure he had heard her.

He shrugged off her question. "Are you happy, Artemisa?"

"At our age, if we are not happy with the life we have made, we might as well die."

"I suppose we should be satisfied," he ventured.

"Listen, viejito," she said, sitting up in the bed. "It's a dog's life any way you look at it. When you are rich, then you dance like a dog, all happy and excited, tongue hanging out, tail wagging. When you're poor, you eat like a dog."

"I'm having lunch with Marcela tomorrow." He chuckled. "She's ordering from Domino's."

"She's poor because she wants to be."

"And we're rich because we want to be rich?"

"No, Carlos. Because God wants us to be. You've never understood that?"

"She's happy."

"Go back to your own bed," she snapped, giving his back a shove with her small fist and then gathering the covers close around her. "I'm happy too. If you can't be happy with me, then maybe you should go live with Marcela."

"Don't take it like that. It was just a comment."

"Buenas noches, Carlitos," she said.

George Rabasa

He nodded, even though she had turned away from him. She heard him leave the room, closing the door very softly behind him. In the morning, she would call Marcela and forgive her. Then she would make a proposition to her: "Your father misses you." She would send her a check to help her rent a bigger place.

The Last Pages

George Rabasa

Writing is the fourth most important thing I do. It ranks after meditating, breathing, and eating.

Sex is up there, too, maybe in seventh or eighth place along with running along the Mississippi River and watching *The Simpsons* on TV.

Unfortunately, I ran out of change for the photo machine and could only get these four shots. And these might be a bit too much. But, after realizing that even better than seeing my words in print is the thrill of stamping my face all over the place, I couldn't resist.

This may be an abuse of the Last Pages.

I thought about this. But then I figured, it's not very often a writer gets a page to do with as the spirit dictates. No editing, no rejections, no apologies.

So here he is, George Rabasa doing live and on camera the four most important things in his life.

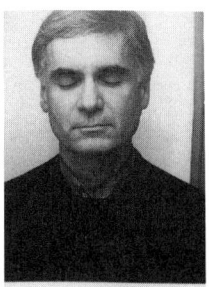

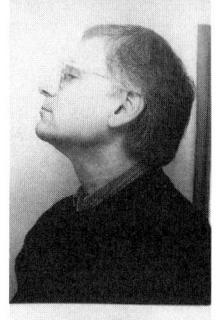

LARA STAPLETON

I chose this photo and the one with my story because my sister Sara is so exquisitely adorable that it wrings my heart. Most kids are cute, but Sara was the kind of child who people want to blow razzberries all over. She wore a bun bigger than her head and had huge ears and the most elated smile.

Now she's a recent graduate of the University of Michigan, with a scholarly inclination toward psychology and linguistics. She's also a great wit and my best friend.

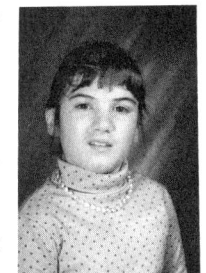

This is the five of us in 1974. We now have an addition to our family, my lovely little sister Annie, who is my blood cousin as well. It is sheer coincidence that I wrote "Joselito" a year before any of this came to pass. This photo was taken ten years before she was even born.

It cracks me up that my brother and I are so all-American in our scout uniforms. We have spent so much of our lives with much more of an outsider's aesthetic, both of us. He is a musician, living in Seattle.

PETE FROMM

Living where I do, long drives are a part of life. In the last few years, I've driven through the INEL several times without getting used to the sinister signs warning of Unexploded Ordnance. But it wasn't until recently that I realized I no longer even glanced at, let alone thought about, the nuclear missile silos dotting the countryside around Great Falls. Wilton and his wife and his work started to take shape at seventy miles an hour, on a stretch of highway dotted with nothing but those orange military signs.

Tony Eprile

My stories often germinate suddenly out of odd, tiny seeds—a chance remark, a glimpse of someone passing by, an offhand observation in a book or newspaper article—and "The Entrepreneurs" is no exception. I had returned to South Africa in 1990 after a prolonged absence. One day, I got into a conversation with a black South African who had what seemed to me a wonderful job as manager of a progressive theater. When he heard that I was living "that side" (the U.S.), he said how much he wished to go there. "What I want to do," he said, "is be a bicycle vendor in New York." Someone had told him that you couldn't buy samosas, the small, curried pastries that are a national snack in South Africa, on the streets of Manhattan, and he saw in this his chance to make a killing.

Traveling through South Africa, I was shocked by the havoc apartheid had wreaked, how *successful* this patently mad policy had been in displacing millions of people and dividing the country—spiritually and in fact. Yet, there was this dynamic Horatio Alger ethos among many black South Africans, who saw the coming years as times of opportunity and triumph over difficult odds. "Spaza shops" and other small businesses proliferated, mostly in the "informal sector" since the people lacked access to the traditional world of commerce, or didn't trust it.

I see "The Entrepreneurs" as very specific to this period in South Africa's history. By the time the story appears in print, Brits Van Stossel may well be out of a job—and then again, he may not. A final note on my protagonist's name: it is in part an homage to Naboth Mokgatle, who wrote *The Autobiography of an Unknown South African*. Naboth of "The Entrepreneurs" is a sort of Everyman, but he's mostly himself. May he prosper!

JANICE LEVY

I hoard others' habits like rare coins: he stirs his coffee with a butter knife; she curls her eyelashes with wet fingertips; the cat cleans his whiskers from left to right. I keep the coins in my pockets and jingle them all day. I feel safe in their weight, sure their value will increase with time.

I look for the limp, the unraveling hem, the tattoo of an ant on an ankle. Sequins from a dancer's navel ruby his cheeks. A pizza kiss stains her chin. In the wink of refrigerator light, their eyes twitch rabbit red.

I listen for the lisp, the honeyed Os, the syllables stiff as iced celery. His voice sounds dangerous, like the rumble of a cycle; hers, as scared as the stutter-cough of rusty wheels. Giggles hiccup; nervous bubbles pop in fluted crystal.

Smells take me places—to leather shoulders wept upon, to the musky V of Grandma's breasts, to blood drying between my thighs in recovery rooms.

A newborn stares at mother, hears her love coos, inhales her scent. Baby sighs, This is easy. To be loved, I need only breathe.

Illusion is the first of all pleasures.

I write because it gives me pleasure. When it doesn't, I will empty my pockets of their coins.

Victoria Lancelotta

There have been places, for me, that as I've walked into them I've immediately started *remembering* them—which is, I suppose, a strange thing, and not déjà vu. What I'm talking about is a kind of lucidity, a hyperclarity of perception that I usually don't encounter until I've been away from a place for a while, and then only if that place held some monumental significance in my life. So there are two ways to go: I either walk into a place, see it, and then remember it; or I walk into a place, begin to "remember" it immediately, and then obsess about it.

There's a place in Baltimore called the Rendezvous Lounge on the corner of Howard and Twenty-fifth streets. I haven't been there in a while and I've heard it's changed—they've taken the booths out and installed a doorman (why, I don't know)—but it's still got Christmas lights up in the window year-round and jars of pickled, well, *things* behind the counter. I don't know if that's any kind of recommendation or not, but for some reason, the place haunts my dreams.

ELIZABETH ONESS

"Rufus" grew out of the years I worked at the Taoist Health Institute, a community clinic in the inner city in Washington, D.C. I lived in the neighborhood where this story is set. So that I could get to graduate school at night during that time, I was given a car with doors that didn't lock, by two wonderful friends, Debra and Kevin O'Reagan. The situation of this story is fictional, but every day at the clinic we were confronted with the problems of homelessness, AIDS, and drug addiction, and I'm interested in how people cope when forced to confront these difficulties.

My husband, Chad, and I were given this Chinese seal by two friends who had spent the better part of a year in China. Abbey and Steven are both acupuncturists—I met them through my work at the clinic—and they had this carved for us as a wedding gift. The handle is a dragon carved in stone and, very fittingly, the characters mean "double happiness."

PAST CONTRIBUTING AUTHORS AND ARTISTS
Issues 1 through 12 are available for eleven dollars each.
(Sorry, Issue 3 is sold out.)

Robert A. Abel • Steve Adams • Susan Alenick • A. Manette Ansay • Margaret Atwood • Kyle Ann Bates • Richard Bausch • Robert Bausch • Charles Baxter • Ann Beattie • Barbara Bechtold • Cathie Beck • Melanie Bishop • Corinne Demas Bliss • Valerie Block • Danit Brown • Gerard Byrne • Jack Cady • Carolyn Chute • Dennis Clemmens • Tiziana di Marina • Stephen Dixon • Michael Dorris • Siobhan Dowd • Mary Ellis • James English • Louise Erdrich • Zoë Evamy • Daniel Gabriel • Louis Gallo • Kent Gardien • Ellen Gilchrist • Peter Gordon • Elizabeth Logan Harris • Marina Harris • David Haynes • Ursula Hegi • Andee Hochman • Jack Holland • Linda Hornbuckle • David Huddle • Stewart David Ikeda • Lawson Fusao Inada • Elizabeth Inness-Brown • Charles Johnson • Wayne Johnson • Elizabeth Judd • Jiri Kajanë • Hester Kaplan • Wayne Karlin • Thomas E. Kennedy • Lily King • Maina wa Kinyatti • Marilyn Krysl • Frances Kuffel • Anatoly Kurchatkin • Jon Leon • Doris Lessing • Christine Liotta • Rosina Lippi-Green • William Luvaas • R. Kevin Maler • Lee Martin • Eileen McGuire • Gregory McNamee • Katherine Min • Mary McGarry Morris • Bernard Mulligan • Abdelrahman Munif • Sigrid Nunez • Joyce Carol Oates • Vana O'Brien • Mary O'Dell • Peter Parsons • Jonathan Raban • Anne Rice • Roxana Robinson • Stan Rogal • Frank Ronan • Elizabeth Rosen • Janice Rosenberg • Kiran Kaur Saini • Libby Schmais • Amy Selwyn • Bob Shacochis • Evelyn Sharenov • Floyd Skloot • Barbara Stevens • William Styron • Liz Szabla • Paul Theroux • Patrick Tierney • Abigail Thomas • Randolph Thomas • Joyce Thompson • Patricia Traxler • Kathleen Tyau • Michael Upchurch • Daniel Wallace • Ed Weyhing • Lex Williford • Gary Wilson • Terry Wolverton • Monica Wood • Christopher Woods • Celia Wren • Jane Zwinger

I want to read them all!

    Australians like to think that they're very proud and free and antiauthoritarian, and I put forward the notion, in this novel, that we continue to be pets, that we still have a child's relationship firstly with our English parents who abused and abandoned us, and then with the United States, who, toward the end of the Second World War, really saved our skins in The Battle of the Coral Sea.
from an interview with Peter Carey by Kevin Bacon and Bill Davis

    Carlos, from across the street, offered her a live chicken to alter his three-piece suit. He stood on her front steps holding a hanger with the suit in one hand and the chicken hanging upside down by the feet in his other hand.
from "Making Ends Meet" by E. Burton

    "I can't join you at the bar because I can't stand for very long. I'm not supposed to move. My size is a problem. Look…" With a sweep of his hand, Dacho invited Juan Angel to view his great bulk. "This is Dacho," he said. "My name is Dacho."
from "Stories from Midday" by Frank Michel

    A powerful emotion welled up in him and pooled, like water in a porcelain bowl. Desperately he wanted to present it to Audrey, but he was so afraid of spilling the liquid that he sat very, very still. The moment tattooed itself into memory, then passed.
from "The Architecture of Grief" by Michael Frank